LAST THINGS

For Guy
with best regards,

Madison

6/15/90

LAST THINGS

A NOVEL BY **MADISON JONES**

LOUISIANA STATE UNIVERSITY PRESS
Baton Rouge and London   1989

98 97 96 95 94 93 92 91 90 89   5 4 3 2 1

Designer: *Laura Roubique Gleason*
Typeface: *Caladonia*
Typesetter: *G & S Typesetters, Inc.*
Printer: *Thomson-Shore, Inc.*
Binder: *John H. Dekker & Sons, Inc.*

Library of Congress Cataloging-in-Publication Data
Jones, Madison, 1925–
    Last things : a novel / by Madison Jones.
      p.   cm.
    "A portion of this novel was first published, in slightly
different form, as 'A beginning,' in the Chattahoochee review, v. 5,
pp. 84–90" — T.p. verso.
    ISBN 0-8071-1549-5 (alk. paper)
    I. Title.
PS3560.0517L3 1989
813'.54—dc19
                                       89-30173
                                       CIP

A portion of this novel was first published, in slightly different form, as "A Beginning," in *The Chattahoochee Review*, V (1985), 84–90.

In parts of the novel, the author has made some use of Wayne Greenhaw, *Flying High: Inside Big-Time Drug Smuggling* (New York, 1984).

The paper in this book meets the guidelines for permanence and durability of the Committee on Production Guidelines for Book Longevity of the Council on Library Resources. ∞

For my dear wife Shailah

LAST THINGS

I

Wendell Corbin's return to Bliss County, a place where he had sworn never again to set foot, was like something fated to be. Even at the time it seemed to him a little bit this way. Later, after the events of that summer, the truth of this was a kind of dark certainty in his mind. A fated thing, a mystery.

Not that Wendell's unbroken five-year absence from this county lacked, in itself, elements of the marvelous. That he, a son of old Hap Corbin, should have gone to college at all; that he should have studied English literature there and finally come to think of himself as a writer; and that at last, with recommendations from his former professors, he should have moved on to graduate school at the state university: all these things verged on the incredible. Therefore this recent event was simply the latest in a succession of marvels.

The practical cause of Wendell's return to Bliss County was one of his professors at graduate school, Dr. Leonard T. (for Tugwell) Rathbone. Rathbone presided over the seminar in Romantic poetry and in the winter quarter Wendell was one of his students.

Rathbone's appearance was not prepossessing. The main reason for this, Wendell thought, was all the hair. He qualified this judgment because it was impossible to be sure whether or not a good close clipping would in fact produce a presentable human being. Rathbone looked like somebody peering out of thick bushes, if bushes could be black and

1

gray, and one imagined that in any other setting he would have been hard to identify. The horn-rimmed glasses that magnified his eyes would have helped some, and so would the (apparent) smallness of his mouth, but these were features too common to really set him apart. Of course when he started talking the problem was solved. There was a great gesturing of hands, alternating with serene intervals when his left hand, closed on his right thumb, restrained all movement but that of his mouth. In these moments his eyes, by a gradual process, would incline to the ceiling, and his voice, directed evidently at the deity, would assume a tone of mystical rapture.

But Rathbone was *alive*: this was what the students said. He was *with it*, and they competed to get into his seminar. So did Wendell, successfully, though his motives were not those of the other students. The announced subject of the seminar was the early Romantic poets but the real, almost the exclusive concentration was William Blake, a poet who was the light (an inaccurate word choice) of Rathbone's life. Wendell had come already to a point in his graduate career where he wanted no sweat at all if possible and from his experience he had concluded that Blake was made for him. Since nobody knew exactly what Blake meant most of the time, he fitted Wendell's skills perfectly. All Wendell had to do was shut his inner eye and start hanging together, along with references to Los and Vala and Rintrah, phrases like *apocalyptic redemption* and *annihilation of selfhood* and *lineaments of eternal imaginative form*. If Wendell was not really a writer he could still concoct a mouthful of stunning Blakean commentary before a person could say *transcendental substitute*.

He had another motive, though, a sort of detached or scientific interest in Rathbone as a person. For one thing, a few casual encounters had awakened in him the hunch, afterwards confirmed, that Rathbone was a heavy user if not an addict. Another thing was simply the particular kind of person Wendell took him for, a kind Wendell found interesting: the con man unawares, whose true victim was himself. This

2

was also confirmed. Just a few hours' close observation of him in those seminars made clear enough what later experience put beyond question, that where Rathbone's ego was involved he could not tell the difference between the truth and a nine-story building. Wendell already had wind of this fact, but after listening to him talk, as Rathbone often did at length, about his personal life, Wendell was certain of it. Rathbone's wife of two years from whom he had recently separated, for instance. If she really was the rigid prude he depicted in such eloquent, and visceral, detail, how in God's name had she come to marry this mountain of hair in the first place? For anybody who attended at all closely, there was more than enough to go on. But if a clincher was needed, there was the prodigious esteem in which he came to hold Wendell's intelligence—partly because of Wendell's skill at retreading the phrases he got from Rathbone's mouth. The greater reason, though, was a deliberate and fairly obvious design that Wendell practiced on him.

Rathbone had been involved and clearly had been bested in a scholarly controversy that he regarded as still very much, in fact thunderously, alive. It had happened in one of those little critical quarterly journals—this one named *Probe*—in which critics refuted each other back and forth. In Blake's poem "The Tyger," there were two lines that read:

> When the stars threw down their spears,
> And water'd heaven with their tears . . .

It was, Wendell guessed, nearly impossible to tell just what these lines meant in themselves, and he would have been willing to let the matter pass. Rathbone was not, however.

In his first *Probe* article Rathbone had spun out the most elaborately obscure explanation that Wendell had ever read of anything, and named it "A Cosmological Quest: Blake's Ultimate Design." Unfortunately the article found its way to one Harmon Litvak at a Missouri college who proceeded to shoot it down in the clearest, and rudest, possible language. Rathbone came back for round two with what amounted only to a rehash (an excellent word choice) of his first article peppered with expressions of scorn for Litvak. The result was predictable. It was just like round one except that the Philistine Litvak was even more devastating in response.

Since then silence on the matter had reigned in the scholarly world but not in Rathbone's seminar, where those lines remained a burning issue and Litvak suffered many a snide reference and humiliating refutation. As far as Wendell knew, he was the only student who saw, or at least desired to exploit, the possibilities in the situation. Moved largely by amusement he dug through all four of those articles and, calling upon his considerable skills, erected in his seminar paper such a fortress of Rathbonean phrases that the sputtering Litvak had no choice but to bow his head and leave the field. He delivered the paper orally and sat back in the praise (even the students were taken in) that he had been confident of. Rathbone put an A + + + on the paper. Wendell noticed, though, without surprise, that he did not suggest Wendell try to publish it, in *Probe* or anywhere else. This was just as well, of course.

That was the real beginning of their relationship, based on Rathbone's barely disguised intellectual esteem. Wendell was fairly often in Rathbone's office listening and nodding to the newest refinements on certain already unintelligible interpretations of Blake. But their relationship achieved a richer maturity when, made entirely confident now by some of Rathbone's remarks, Wendell let it out that he was sympathetic with the drug culture. This was when Rathbone first told Wendell to call him Tug, and after that he went on to indicate, rather darkly, that he could put Wendell onto a good source if Wendell wanted. A few days afterward he invited Wendell to meet him, late in the afternoon, for a drink at Finley's Inn, which was a joint with a bar just outside the Drayton city limits. Wendell did so and met Rathbone's girl, Alice, who also had hair—very black and lots of it, though none of it on her face.

She was around thirty, maybe ten years younger than Rathbone, and in spite of a rather stunned expression was

4

not bad to look at. At first Wendell thought that the stunned expression meant *stoned*, but learning that she too had just come from a day's teaching at the university he concluded rightly that this was her natural face. After a couple of drinks she perked up a little and the party became cordial enough so that, at the end, Wendell received another invitation. It was not for drinks, though. It was an invitation to take a room in their house in Turnbull, which was just across the line in Bliss County, a twenty-minute drive.

The invitation did not surprise him nearly as much as did the location of their house. But why this surprise? Wendell was perfectly conscious that for seven months now, ever since he had moved a hundred miles upstate from Goodwin College, he had been living not many miles from his old home county and that some professors as well as students had residences in Turnbull. He was surprised, he thought, because, upon receiving this invitation, he was suddenly visited by the notion that a pursuing destiny had caught and was about to transport him back to the place, or almost the place, of his origins.

His first answer was a firm No. He had left Bliss County determined never to come back, not even briefly or for any reason. He had not even wanted to hear any news from there, and in fact he never had except once, when he got the report that his mother was dead. It did not bring him back. Let the dead, and his brothers—if they were not in jail by now—bury the dead. Now came this invitation, like a summons somehow.

He refused but afterwards he began to think about it. Three weeks later, at the end of March and the conclusion of a mental process in which one by one all his nebulous reasons for refusing got themselves rejected, he said Yes. Turnbull itself was not his home place anyway, even if he had known it fairly well when he was a boy. Besides, he was a different person now, cut loose, a stranger in that county. If, as he had in a sort of twilight way imagined, the place was a trap, what exactly was the nature of the trap? Where was it?

There was also this, which grew in importance as he thought about it more. He was a writer. Look at writers, look at James Joyce. Where else were they to turn but back to the world they knew best of all.

Of course Wendell had a couple of less cloudy reasons for his decision. One of them was his little room in a decaying house full of rancid odors and ungodly music and other noises. Another and greater reason was his desire for any change at all from the desperate tedium of his routine. Graduate school and especially those freshman English classes that his fellowship required him to teach were killing him, and it was getting worse. The ranks of bland bored freshman faces and jaws working away at their gum set his teeth grinding. Chew, you little heifer, he would think, glaring at a half-averted and wholly unfocused female face. But it was still worse in his office with his weekly themes to grade, dozens and dozens of them, lying there in patient expectation on his desk. Grade me.

Bats

Bats are like mice with wings only they dont have any eyes or tales. You might think they would hit things when they fly but they dont they have radar. You cant here it but they can and dodge things. Women specialy are scared of bats, they get in there hare.

Wendell would sit there breaking pencil points and tearing holes among their run-on sentences and prodigies of general fat-headedness. Stopping to blow he would look out his window, high up in historic Tyson Center, and think what a waste of grazing land was all that green lawn cluttered with ugly buildings. Peaceful green, with cows. Or lacking that, how about a nice deep nuclear crater where it all was? Every day was like the end, or at least a single arm's reach from the end, of his rope. Yet he continued to hang on, hoping now that a change of residence would give a little relief, maybe comic relief, to his aching boredom.

6

II

Wendell was well enough pleased with both Turnbull and Rathbone's house. Of course he was already fairly familiar with Turnbull, but now, after five years, he saw it with somewhat different eyes. For one thing it seemed smaller. The two blocks, roughly, of downtown stores and the fact that one could drive straight through town and out the other side in four or five minutes impressed him for the first time with what a little place it really was. It also seemed spruced up a bit, and the houses, at least those along the principal streets, appeared nicer, more venerable. He had never before paid much attention to them and he was surprised to notice that a few of the older and larger houses, like the one next door to Rathbone's, probably dated back to antebellum times. There was of course a black part of town where many of the houses were little better than shacks, but even this part had a certain nostalgic charm. Or so it seemed to him now. As far as he could tell, nothing had been added to the town except a few unremarkable houses, a considerable expansion of Mr. Jason Farrow's lot full of shiny new automobiles, and a museum of local history that because it was housed in an old isolated building at the edge of town was barely noticeable. He did notice it, though, but only in that he had never thought of Turnbull as having a history.

Rathbone's house in style and venerableness was no match for the one next door but it was an old spacious two-story frame with some charm of its own, a charm not diminished by the fact that it was much in need of painting and fixing up both outside and in. Or so he felt to start with. Later the general debility of things got mixed in as an added cause of the disgust he felt for the slovenliness of the life lived in that house.

In the beginning, though, Wendell was well content with just about everything, including even the presence of Rathbone and his lady. He had a big upstairs room all to himself, on a back corner and isolated. The side window looked out on pecan trees much taller than the house and on an expanse of yard that would be all in shade when the trees leafed out and that was bounded at the property line by a tall palisade of privet hedge. Through spaces between the pecan branches he could see over the hedge the house next door and the back gallery where the inhabitants—mostly the woman, who from this distance looked pretty good—sometimes appeared. On the other side of Rathbone Manor was a thicketed vacant lot. Visible from his rear window was an extensive stretch of yard that, beyond another big pecan, a peach, two dogwood trees, and a chicken house, included a sizable garden area where he could see a few vines left over from last year and beginning to sprout. Beyond that was a line of trees and not a house in sight. He had some hours of pleasure in it all and he wondered at the reluctance that had haunted his decision.

But this contentment was not very durable and a week or so left it already severely qualified. He certainly had not expected that daily association with Rathbone and his Lady Alice would be all laughs for him—inward laughs, of course—or that they would be always gratifying his literary appetite with small epitomes of character. But he had expected more, and more interesting specimens in these categories and he had not expected to suffer in their presence anything like the combination of boredom and vexation that he experienced so much of the time.

For one thing Rathbone would not shut up about Blake, even at breakfast when most people were naturally in a bad humor. Wendell was no longer in his seminar but now he had Rathbone for breakfast and supper and also those interminable daily automobile rides back and forth to Drayton, enough on the subject of Blake to dry up his brains. To cap it all, there were those many times when Rathbone, usually smoking a joint, would enter his room at night and capture him, leaving behind a punky smell when he finally departed. It was in the potted state, Wendell observed, that Rathbone derived his original ideas and Wendell began to wonder about the effects on him of a different drug, whether it might possibly produce ideas with a little more clarity. Or, which would be far the best, no ideas at all. Wendell thought about this.

With some silence and a little cleanliness breakfast could have been so pleasant in that kitchen. Spring broke just a few days after Wendell had moved in and the early sun shone on the back stoop, and the dogwood trees in the yard were all white with bloom. With the door open the bird songs were loud in the kitchen and one could smell the fresh earth turning green. That is, if one could have shut Rathbone out. Bent hump-shouldered over his bowl of grits (though a northerner he had developed a gargantuan passion for grits), he did not permit even the biggest mouthful to stifle his voice for more than a second or two. "'Every child may joy to hear,'" he would say, through grits, referring to the vernal morn. "Deceptive, though. The realm of generation—Tirzah, Blake named it—is always waiting . . ." He took another mouthful, which broke his pace for a second. ". . . to enslave the spirit. Tirzah the home of Urizen, the bleak rational, static negation. Where we all live now. I was thinking last night, Wendell . . ."

Wendell, because his brains were reeling, was trying not to think, but Rathbone was sitting directly across the table from him. In this instance, though, a distraction intervened. Wendell noticed that his wrist was stuck to the oilcloth and, snatching it loose, he was off on another of his trains of angry thought about the sloppiness of their lives. Just a few whisks of a wet rag would have fixed it—no sweat, and no arm stuck to the table. Unimportant, though: which is what both of them would have said, with a haughty air, if Wendell had ever raised the question. Which is what they would have said if he had mentioned the general disorder of the house, the dust and books and papers lying everywhere and broken furniture and the horrific state of their own bedroom that looked as if a bomb exploded in it. Wendell thought he would never understand how they managed to come up with clothing fit to wear in public. But they did, if just barely in Rathbone's case. Alice, on school mornings anyway, always appeared on the scene turned out in quite acceptable style.

Wendell did not think that Alice, though seated barely an arm's length away, had more than peripheral consciousness, if even that, of Rathbone's table talk and he sometimes wondered how Rathbone got along before he came on the scene. He had long since become satisfied that Alice's stunned expression was simply nature and not a result of the previous night's always heavy indulgence in pot. But she had good features, large dark mysterious eyes, and lips that, if remarkably pale, were full and nicely chisled, and black black hair that fell nearly to her waist in back. Though much too thin—she was anorexic, he decided—her body was well shaped and rather statuesque, a consciousness of which had probably inspired her habit of sitting anywhere with a prim erectness that was like a second contradiction of her generally sloppy ways. That was how she sat at the kitchen table, erect but surely not attentive, picking forgetfully at her food and, one supposed, pursuing in spite of her lover's portentous voice her own private and probably eerie reflections.

Alice's last name was Shulty but whether or not that was her name from a marriage Wendell did not find out. Probably it was, it made no difference. For what was in a name— or a marriage either, for that matter. He supposed that if she and Rathbone had been married and thereby conscious of legal bonds on their freedom the arguments between them would have been worse than they were.

They were bad enough. Anything could trigger them but the most likely cause was some word or act of Rathbone's that could be interpreted as expressive of sexist attitudes. In certain atmospheres a question from Rathbone such as "Has the mailman come?" was quite enough to strike fire. Her head would dart forward like chicken snake's and in a tight voice she would demand to know why a deliverer of mail could not be a woman as well as a man. Rathbone, always dignified to start with, would reply that he had seen this mailperson and it was a man. But even so definitive a reply was no inconvenience for Alice: not so much as a pause retarded her answer. Rathbone, she declared, in any case would *assume* that it was male—he always assumed this, always. The consequent denial came to naught and the argument would go on scaling upward to the stage at which they began to describe each other in phrases like "the anal-oral type" (Rathbone) and "the type of the specious and sterile rational" (Alice).

In the actual case of the mailman dispute Wendell tried to mitigate things with the lightsome observation that "mailperson," which sounded the same as "maleperson," would not be acceptable either. This was his one such slip. Alice looked at him with the most withering contempt and called him "a fucking little slimeball."

Such were the causes of Wendell's early discontent but still he was happier, by a little, than when he had been confined in his room in Drayton. There were quiet times in the house, particularly when, as often happened, both Alice and Rathbone had stoned themselves into utter speechlessness. At such times especially he wrote a little, though he seemed still unable to keep anything going. He enjoyed late evenings in the garden preparing ground and setting out plants and, for the first week or two, he enjoyed walking around town. Of the four or five antebellum-style houses in Turnbull, much the nicest was the one next door to Rathbone's house. It was not only painted a radiant white, it had a grace about it that, he concluded, resided mainly in the two pairs of tall slim columns flanking the narrow front porch and supporting a latticed balcony at the second-floor level. It also housed a lady who he wanted a closer look at than he had so far managed.

There was another kind of thing that Wendell, in his own

way, enjoyed. Once a week or so Rathbone gave a party—though *gave* was maybe not the right word for a gathering at which the guests just appeared in the most random way, at any hour and as likely as not by means of the back door, bringing their own hooch or pot or whatever else they found to be spiritually elevating. Most of them were professors from various departments of the university, one or two of whom also had residences in Turnbull. There were, however, to Wendell's surprise, a few local people unconnected with the university—people who, he at first mistakenly supposed, must have lived their daily lives in the presence of a whole townful of cold shoulders. There was much shuffling about and laughter and hot arguments, together with intervals of discourse so high that every head was spellbound. Later there would be a few inert bodies sprawled or draped on pieces of furniture here and there, and people would disappear for a while and then return, and pot groups would form themselves in hushed ceremonial circles on the floor like Indians communing with the Spirit.

Wendell's fun was in the observing, though to appear *with it* he sometimes indulged in a little pot or whiskey. Never much. He was busy taking the measure of these people, taking them into his memory, from which someday they would step forth as characters in a blistering comic novel. Clowns, fools, self-deceivers, serviceable knaves: the whole cast was here. Yet where in his whole life, he more and more often reflected, had he encountered people really deserving of exclusion from all these categories?

He was ruminating about this one day when he happened to meet the lady from next door and for a little while he was thinking, Here's one, maybe. It was a late evening in the garden, just when the bullbats were starting to fly. He was watering the tomato plants he had put out and when he finished emptying the can and turned around he saw her. The boundary hedge was sparse back here and she was visible through a gap, standing in her own well-tended garden with a trowel in her hand. She spoke first and he took a polite few steps closer.

12

"You're the graduate student, aren't you . . . living with Dr. Rathbone?"

"Yes ma'm," Wendell said. First twilight a little dimmed his scrutiny of her and he got the immediate impression of a woman ten years younger than the thirty-eight or -nine she turned out to be. In that light with the strands of gray invisible, her hair looked more blond than it was and her skin as creamy smooth as a schoolgirl's. She fitted those jeans she wore and if there was an ampleness of breast and hips and butt it did not noticeably exceed the amplitudes of the coeds they were breeding these days. And there were the teeth, a moving-picture smile.

"I'm Tricia Harker," she said, still smiling, " . . . your neighbor from over the hedge."

He took a deep breath and said, "I'm glad to know you," and then, bethinking himself, "I'm Wendell . . . Corbin." Something that stirred in his mind had enfeebled his utterance of his last name and now he realized what it was, the name itself. This after all was Bliss County and names were known. Those trashy Corbins. But he did not see this in her face or hear it when she said,

"You talk like us homefolks. I always think of graduate students as coming from way off someplace."

"I'm from Georgia," he lied, as naturally as if it had been true. Henceforth it would be true. "Not much difference in the way we talk over there." He would spell his name with a k . . . and maybe an e. He was still in thrall.

Wendell's thralldom was short-lived, however. Given his cold habits of discernment he was not one to be manipulated overmuch by purely glandular excitements. When, after a few more introductory pleasantries, she turned the conversation to intellectual matters the scales began to fall from his eyes. She was *into* Nietzsche, for God's sake, following, probably from over her kitchen table, in the tracks of that old housewife-befuddler Zarathustra. She kept using the word *Ubermensch*, pitching it in the voice of somebody who had detected a rare bird in one of her shade trees. ("I looked up and there was an Ubermensch.")

"And to think," she said, "about just turning your back on all the things other people think are *good*." This gave her a little shudder, right down to the trowel in her hand. But it was all just so *fascinating*. "Of course we're church members, even if we don't go very much, and we don't believe God's dead or anything. I don't think I do," she said, displaying a moment of self-doubt. "But just to think about ideas like that, the kind of person an Ubermensch would be."

By then Wendell wished he was an Ubermensch, one high up in a tree. Or else one of those bullbats overhead—a creature anyway more appropriate to the occasion—whose darting courses his gradually uplifted eyes had begun to follow. If there had been any scales left to fall they certainly would not have withstood her spiel about *her* family and how religious they were and how shocked they would have been at these ideas. In fact all this was a transparent digression designed to color her boasting about her (or her husband's?) aristocratic *forebears*. " . . . a chaplain in the Confederate army," she was saying. "He's the one that built our house," gesturing with the trowel toward the house, " . . . in 1856. He died at the battle of Chickamauga. . . . And here *I* am studying Nietzsche," she concluded, with a smile mixed of wonder and sad self-denigration.

She wanted them to have a talk and was already pressing for an appointed time, when good fortune struck. A male voice calling from her invisible back gallery announced that she was wanted for something evidently urgent, something that made her compress her lips. But it released Wendell and in the following days he did a little careful scouting before he went out to tend his garden.

He met somebody else about this time. He was walking past Farrow's big car lot that was on the left just after one came into town on the Drayton road and he had got fairly close, too close, before he noticed the young black man looking at him. The man was standing just inside the lot with a cloth in one hand and the other hand on the fender of a shiny new Pontiac. The man was Cat Bird.

Wendell was anything but glad to see him. His habit was

to turn aside from any face that looked as if it even might be familiar and this meeting with Cat was especially unpleasant. But now there was nothing to do except take those last few steps and speak to him.

"What're you doing down here at Turnbull, Cat," he said, trying to keep his voice from reflecting anything. "Buying you a car?"

Cat's expression passed through a crooked grin. "You back, huh?"

"Just for a while. Living with a friend for a while."

Except for an almost white scar under his left eye Cat had not changed at all. His expressions came and went, he shifted his feet, and now he began to swing the cloth back and forth in his hand. "Schoolboy," he finally said, just saying the word to himself. Then, to Wendell, "Can't stop being a schoolboy."

Wendell wondered how Cat knew this but he only said, "I'm going to stop pretty soon. Then I'm heading out."

"Yeah? Out where?"

Something at a distance in back of Cat had obscurely caught Wendell's attention. It was not, as he at first thought, merely the sudden fluttering in a breeze of the little orange banners festively suspended on strings across the car lot. Whatever it was continued to happen while he answered Cat's question, saying, "Anywhere. Just *out*. Maybe Atlanta."

"Yeah. Atlanta, huh?"

Now Wendell knew what had distracted him, pressing, as it seemed, at the margin of his consciousness. It was surely a meaningless trivial thing but it was one that in those moments had a vaguely distressing effect. The car agency building with its plate-glass front was not very far away. The noon angle of sunlight glazed without quite blinding the glass and made obscure the interior of the building and also the single figure that stood there watching—watching Wendell. Or so he was convinced, though the figure visible through the glass was as featureless as a paper cut-out. For a few seconds of great intensity Wendell stared, trying to make the face come clear.

"It's work for you here," Cat said. "Money, man. Getting

bigger." A grin, passing as Wendell's eyes came back to his face, gave way to a glance Wendell remembered well—that glance that was quick and cold and impossible to read.

"Not for me," Wendell said, still feeling his distress.

The figure in the plate-glass window had vanished. Besides this, by a stroke of luck, somebody was approaching, two old men coming along the sidewalk. Wendell lifted a hand in final salute to Cat and headed up the street. Within a minute or two he was past Danford's Corner and out of sight; but it was days before he could get this little encounter cleanly out of his mind.

III

It was clear to Wendell that even as a very small boy he had been no real part of his family. His mother's sensing this fact must have been the main reason she was fond of predicting dire things for him, the most common being that he would end up in the devil's clutches. She told him many times that even in his cradle, where he yelled and kicked and fidgeted more than all his brothers and sisters put together, it was as if he was trying to show how much he disliked everything around him. There was no other reason, he was never sick. Just born that way, she said, and went on to add that he took after a brother of hers whom Wendell had never laid eyes on in his life. So, as Wendell later concluded, it was a matter of plain genetic inheritance, because he could not in early infancy have been rebelling against what he was born into—such as the apple or other kind of crate that no doubt was his cradle.

Whether or not his dissatisfaction was inborn, there were, after he had had time to develop human good sense, more than enough reasons for its origin. As he saw it the first reason was his parents, the second was his brothers and sisters, and the third was all the kinfolks with whom he had ever had any acquaintance. To say only that they were short on brains was woefully inadequate. In a few of them, like his mother, there was a certain canniness, but nothing that anybody in his right mind would call real intelligence. Therein was a puzzle. How did Wendell, who was always considered uncommonly bright, manage to get born into such a clan? Again, genetic accident, the same kind of accident that presumably explained why he had never laid eyes on that maternal uncle of his. Clearly he and the uncle had been awfully lucky, because it was quite a stunt for those genes. In all the family talk Wendell had ever heard, there was never once an indication of a single deceased family member who appeared, on the evidence, to have had even a knee up on present generations.

Intelligence and backbone went best together but there was such a thing as the latter without the former. Except Wendell's mother up to a point, his family did not have backbone either. All the male kin he knew about—including his three brothers as long as they were around—barely hung on to jobs as farm laborers or pulpwooders or handymen at stores in and around Bison Springs and Turnbull. He never knew more than one or two of them to get a promotion, to clerk or anything else. The females, including his two sisters, all got married to men not much up the scale from his brothers and his father and settled down or moved away to repeat the same dismal process of generation.

Wendell's father was if anything a cut beneath the least of his children. There was a time Wendell barely remembered when his father owned some property, thirty-eight acres with a house, sort of, two miles southwest of Bison Springs. He got hold of it through almost the only stroke of luck ever to befall any of his family: his wife won an automobile in a lottery and sold it for enough money to buy the place. The result was four or five years of scrounging to keep off the tax collector and then the quite predictable occurred. After that it was Mr. Haney Cartwright's big farm where the family lived in a house that must have cost seventy-five dollars brand new and where every family member was supposed to be farm help. On that farm and in that house was where Wendell spent most of his youth.

It was not a happy youth, though the place did have some pleasant features. The house, or cabin, sat on a low knoll with a view of a big green pasture in front, and nearby there was a deep creek to swim and fish in. But the walls of the house did not do a thing but shred the winter wind and when there was no wind, smoke from the two chunkrock fireplaces was so thick that they had to keep the windows open or choke to death. Besides this the house was too little for the family. Wendell, the youngest, and his three brothers slept in a room that would have crowded one pair of midgets, and his sisters and his parents were not much better off in their own rooms. Of course there was never enough money. The family diet (he remembered best a pot of white beans heated over and over again and added to every few days) should have given them all permanent cases of the rickets, and almost the only clothes any of the children ever had came from some such place as the Goodwill Store.

Wendell could have put up with these things, though, if it had not been for the character of his family. By the time he was eight he had already begun to look at them with a cold eye, and it grew colder. The first thing he could remember being embarrassed about was the names of his brothers. By God knew what freakish inspiration of his parents the boys were named Majer, Miner, and Fawbus, in that order. Wendell felt that he (he had later added the second l to his name) had somehow come off fairly well, though in that house he was never called anything but Bubba. His sisters' names, Ramona and Ronda, seemed, if only by contrast with his brothers', also not too bad. He tried to forget that his brothers even had names.

But this little embarrassment was only the beginning. Before long, at least at school, he was also trying to forget that he had any brothers. This was impossible. Their stupidity alone was enough to guarantee that they would be always on display. Although he was by three years the younger, he caught up with Fawbus in the fifth grade. He caught up with Miner in the seventh and was saved from catching up with Majer only by the fact that Majer turned sixteen, the age at which he was legally permitted to quit school.

But his brothers were on display also by reason of their incorrigible rowdiness. Spitballs, stinkbombs, snakes turned loose in the classrooms, thumbtacks planted in the seats of desks: whatever the uproar the principal went looking first for Wendell's brothers while Wendell, hunkered at his desk, labored to be oblivious to it all. It was no use. If nothing else his brothers themselves kept him reminded of their bond. They were always hailing him in the halls or on the playground, or from inside the principal's office, where they spent half their time, or on the way out as they headed home on another three-day suspension. Hate might have been too strong a word for what Wendell felt, but shame and outrage were not—a shame and an outrage that at one intensity or another were always with him.

At home, where there was no rational eye but his own to observe them, it was less bad for Wendell, if bad enough. Majer and Miner, who were barely a year apart, were always getting into fistfights, usually because one of them had lost something and accused the other of having taken it. Wendell's mother would stand there screaming at them, and Fawbus and the girls would cry and Wendell's father, without even getting up from the decomposing cane rocker he always sat in, would lift his voice in a stream of loud steady cussing. If there had been anybody within a quarter of a mile he surely would have called the sheriff, but there was nobody. Wendell always took off for the creek and stayed awhile, maybe taking a few of those deep dives he loved into the underwater silence, and when he came back everything would be not only over with but forgotten. It would be really forgotten—no red faces or sniping or any signs of disgruntlement. That fight might just as well have happened a week before.

This forgetting, Wendell thought, had nothing to do with goodness of heart. It was simply a spectacular lack of attention span that the whole family except him shared, if not in quite equal parts. He thought that his father had the largest share. The old boy (Hap, people called him) was just barely capable of forming habits. One of his chores was to milk Mr. Cartwright's cows morning and evening seven days a week, yet every so often for no reason he would just forget to. "Plumb slipped my mind," he would say. He would forget to close gates and have to spend hours driving the cows back in, and he would walk away and leave a tractor motor idling all night. "A man can't think of ev'ything." Wendell was always worrying about his losing his job, until he realized the cause and extent of Mr. Cartwright's tolerance. Where else could Mr. Cartwright find a hand who was a big enough fool to do even the kind of work Wendell's father did for beggar's wages and use of a shack that never had to be repaired.

In a family like that, Wendell was naturally looked on as downright weird. The lesser reason was his relentless and often raging pursuit of privacy: after his earliest years he had practically stopped talking to members of the family except when compelled to. The greater reason was his strange love of reading. He not only read constantly, he even owned some books which he kept like treasure, under wraps, in a corner of his shared room. With no other escape in that house he submerged himself in the world those books gave him, where people, however curious or depraved, had more sense in a minute than his whole family did in a year. He became so good at submerging himself that he did not even hear what passed for conversation around him. Sometimes he did not even hear the fights. To bring him out they usually had to shake him and when he looked up, there would be one or another of them looking at him the way a person would have watched Lazarus emerging from the tomb. He was something for them to roll their heads about and he did not know how many times he had heard his father say, "That there boy's the first un ever knowed in my whole connection to read aer book." And he might add, though not directly in Wendell's presence, "Them books is what makes him so funny."

His weirdness made them uneasy and also angry sometimes, but it was not hard to detect a buried measure of respect among their feelings: he was, after all, a prodigy among them. His father, though he did well to spell out words on a road sign, for some reason especially felt this way. He used to tell Wendell that once upon a time he had known how to read real good too but that somewhere along the way he had just forgot how. Then, maybe, he would ask Wendell to read him something from one of the books. The result was always the same. Wendell would read a paragraph or two and suddenly the old boy would lift his burnt-red hand and tell him to stop, that was enough. All them words: he didn't understand none of them. But he would be looking at Wendell in a certain way, blinking as at a miracle enacted there before him. This was the closest any family member ever came to open acknowledgment of Wendell's gifts, and it was the basis for the only bond he ever felt with any of them.

This was the basis but it was a change of circumstances that allowed the bond to grow as strong as it did—which was not really very strong, or durable. At fourteen Wendell was the only child left at home, and that was one thing. Another was that by this time his father had developed rheumatism and instead of being out at work he spent most of his days sitting or lying around the house groaning. Mr. Cartwright let him stay on: who else would live there? So Wendell not only saw more of his father than in the past, he also had to listen to his groans. These groans got seriously on his nerves and finally drove him to a step that turned out to be a very important, in fact a fateful one—and not only for his relations with his father.

Wendell's brothers, before and after leaving home, were always smoking pot. For the simple reason that *they* did he had never done so, but he had heard enough from them to know where it could be bought. One day, a day when his father was groaning even more than usual, he happened to read in a magazine that pot was good for such as rheumatism. He walked the two miles to Bison Springs and located a young Negro named Cat Bird, whom he had heard his brothers mention, and with money he had been hoarding bought a nickel bag. That started it. Once he had taught his father to take and hold a few drags off the cigarette he had rolled for him, their little bond was formed. It was a mutual dependency as strong on his part as on his father's, curiously, and it lasted for several years. That was the nearest he had ever come to participating in a friendship. Wendell thought that if his father had had anything at all in his head their relationship might possibly have blossomed into something that would have changed his fate.

But this was to exaggerate a little. The old boy did have *something* in his head, some old dusty and fragmented memories that were almost the only subject of conversation between them. These were conversations that, somehow, Wendell remembered warmly, especially the ones on the front porch, from which certain floorboards were perilously missing, in mild weather when they sat looking out over the green pasture where whiteface cows were grazing in the sun. If it was early spring the thicket of plum bushes that was closing in on the house were white with bloom, and so with the dogwoods in the fence row just out front.

Occasionally his mother would, in a way of speaking, join them, sitting on what was left of the steps to shell a bucket of peas. But she never said anything much except once in a while when she made a pious observation or corrected in an irritable voice a slip in her husband's recollections. Physically she was almost his exact opposite, a low fat woman with no neck at all. Wendell's father, leaning back in that unraveling cane rocker, looked like a just-living body loosely held together by hooks at all his joints. His neck was extraordinarily long and on top of it was a little ball of a head from which all but a rim of gray hair had vanished. There was nearly as much hair in his big flaplike ears, but this was yellow from all the wax he never thought to remove. His skin, of course, face and crown and neck and hands, was a permanent burnt-red. He was essence of Redneck.

From these conversations Wendell learned all he ever would know about his ancestors—which was not much and hardly worth knowing. As best he could discover, not one of them had ever amounted to anything. Most of them seemed to have spent their misbegotten lives losing things and almost getting things they did not get and having children and accidents and violent encounters. "My uncle Floyd," his father said, "didn't have no right arm at all. Lost hit in old Mr. Buck Rainer's cotton gin. Tore hit plumb right off at the shoulder. Biggest mess I ever seen."

This was only one of what must have been a dozen uncles. Another one, called Wedge, was even more unlucky. "Taken out after that nigger, gonna kill him. Nigger shot him in the foot. Wedge drug hisself back home till he got well, and taken out after that nigger again. Nigger shot him in the head. They ain't ketched that nigger yet."

Another uncle, though, had come very close to being actually lucky. He had almost inherited a hundred acres, from an old widow who had taken a shine to him and aimed to put him down in her will. Shirt-tail close, he come. That widow dropped dead on the way to the lawyer to put her name on that paper. Wendell's father would shake his round little head. His only memory, apparently, of real luck among his kin was of a now-dead sister of his who, after eight other children, had triplets and got a picture of herself and the babies on page two of the *Bliss County Weekly News*.

The old boy's memories, such as they were, ranged back through two generations of his family and stopped right there as if against a blank wall that was where human history had its beginning—nothing on the other side. It was as if his grandfather's generation had been set down in Bliss County like Adam and Eve already full grown and shaped the way they were and the way they always would be. Around about through the county, there were a few of the old antebellum houses still surviving, standing there like reminders. Except his bad luck that he was not born in one of them, they did not remind Wendell's father of anything. His memories, though limited to the same stretch of countryside that contained these houses, afforded only passing glimpses of them. That the houses were supposed to remind people of a vanished and different way of life was something Wendell had to learn from books, because nothing he heard his father recall suggested that this was true. Instead of an Eden to start with, there was nothing but a dark backward and abysm of time.

Wendell's father did not seem to regard his haphazard portrait of things past as especially bleak: the bleakness was just life. Sometimes, as when he told about a particualrly heartbreaking failure of luck or a gruesome accident, he would even show a certain zest for that life. His voice would break out of its monotone and rise a little and he might bob his head and clench his knees with his loose bony fingers. Such an outburst was usually followed by an extended period of reverie and after that he would want a few more drags off the now-burnt-out reefer he probably had dropped to the floor.

The pot did him good and, Wendell was sure, had nothing to do with causing the stroke that finally hit him. One day Wendell tried it himself and shared with his father that little interval of silly laughter and after that the stopping of time and the comical way that words and meanings kept escaping from his grasp. It was like a little holiday. People, especially people like his father, needed such holidays and he began to reflect on what a shame and more than a shame it was that the law pursued and put people in jail because of pot. Stupid. Maybe because his brothers had such a hatred of the law, being always in trouble with it, Wendell had never before had any such feelings. He began to now, and his hostility grew stronger. Partly in defiance he started taking those little holidays pretty often, himself, and finally he even got some seed and grew a few plants in the woods down by the creek. This gave him a good deal of satisfaction. It was also the beginning of his rebellion—his usually discreet and prudent rebellion—against established things.

IV

His father's stroke put an end to the existence of anything that Wendell could specifically call *home*. Twelve miles from Bison Springs, not very far out of Turnbull, was a state-operated Home For The Infirm and that was where they put his father, permanently. His mother and he went to live with one of her sisters thirty-five miles away in Upjohn County but Wendell did not last long there. His aunt took an immediate dislike to him, a dislike he returned, and after about three weeks he came back to Bison Springs and moved in, reluctantly, with his sister Ramona and her husband. He lived there for two years, until he graduated from high school and, by means of a college scholarship he won, finally shook the dust of Bliss County from his shoes.

Of course he had to pay something for living in Ramona's house. Each week he handed her husband—Bleep, they called him—seven dollars, which was Bleep's drinking money and which Wendell earned at various odd jobs. He lived in a tiny room on the back of their tiny frame house and stayed as clear as he could of both of them. This was not clear enough. Ramona had a bad temper and a loud braying voice to go with it and she and Wendell had regular clashes that almost but never quite resulted in his getting booted out. The real reason this did not happen was the value Bleep put on that seven dollars a week. The money he made with his pulpwood truck was not enough to keep his insides oiled.

Wendell's odd jobs varied but there was one he finally hit on and stuck with until he left the county. This was hustling pot. He was very subtle and successful at it. He got in with

Cat Bird, who was by now a wholesaler with apparently large and obviously mysterious connections. Wendell paid him usually two-thirds of what he got on the streets and country roads in and around Bison Springs and Turnbull, keeping a surprisingly generous one-third for himself. He made a good deal of money but he also fancied the work. It helped him arrive at a settled view of things, himself included.

Of course he was not always on the job. His current ambition in life was to part company not only with Bliss County but with all his family and kin forever and the most promising means he could strike on was to win that scholarship available at school. He redoubled his scholarly efforts. Because of all his reading he was already far out ahead of his bumpkin classmates and now he found himself making fools of them—which they resented and he enjoyed. He discovered that his teachers were also ignoramuses but he kept this discovery under his hat until, in the middle of his senior year, he had the scholarship nailed down. After that, with a kind of systematic enjoyment, he let them feel it. In the end they were as glad as his classmates were to see the last of him.

Since then a lot of people had been glad to see the last of him but it was not because he repeated his high-school mistake. After all, his teachers, having become his enemies, did teach him something. Realizing that the enmity he had gratuitously inspired had sullied his good name around Bison Springs, he did some profitable reflecting. What he came up with was this: Keep your contempt to yourself, because sneers and laughter could cost much more than they're worth. It was a truth too obvious to be denied and he set out, with regret, to make it habitual practice. The regret was wasted, though, for there was a corollary truth that he soon discovered. It was that the pleasure of sneers and laughter need not suffer diminishment in a man's secret mind. The opposite, in fact. He came to learn that laughter spilled lost its special savor.

Books and hustling pot were the good part of his life in

those two years. As for the rest, it was just about of a piece with his earlier life. He had never had any friends and the situation was no different now, unless one could count his off-and-on flirtation with a timid pigtailed girl named May Sikes, whom he walked home from school sometimes. Not that he had anything in mind. It had not occurred to him, yet, to actually try laying hands on a girl: mostly they just walked along in silence. This was typical of his human relations. If he had ever had anything like real conversations with anybody they were those stoned ones on the rotten front porch of their old cabin. It was a measure of his loneliness that these conversations in much altered form and circumstances still continued, for until he left for college he occasionally went to visit his father at the Home.

It was not clear to him why he went. Even the place, the unshaded raw-brick building that resembled a manufacturing concern, was unpleasant. The sterile hall he had to pass through was always crowded with dessicated figures in wheelchairs who watched him with empty eyes or, recognizing him as somebody else, summoned him with urgent gestures. His father in his own wheelchair was invariably positioned in the doorway to his room, exactly balanced, as it were, across the threshold. He would look at Wendell noncommittally when Wendell bent to push him back inside and he would continue to watch while Wendell sat down on the bed and uttered a brief greeting. Then would come the uncertain moment in which Wendell waited to see whether anybody at all was at home today. The old boy was not greatly changed. His pale blue eyes had never had much life and his loose-fingered hands had always been pretty well nerveless. The main difference Wendell noticed was that his mouth hung open and that the coloring of his skin had declined from the old burnt-red to a kind of unwholesome pink.

Some days his father would speak, though in broken phrases, recalling his dismal memories of uncles and aunts and cousins that he had used to treat Wendell to on the front porch. Although he never called Wendell by name, Wendell took these fragments of recollection as assurance that the old man recognized him. On some occasions there was greater assurance. Then, with index and second finger held uncertainly apart, his father would lift his hand as though he had a reefer in it and put the hand to his mouth. Those moments always moved Wendell. And always, afterwards, he would experience an interval of barely stifled anger. More than once he considered bringing some pot in with him and, behind the closed door, helping the old man to smoke it. It was too risky. He settled for the conclusion that his father's wits were already cloudy enough to keep him pretty serene.

In spite of Wendell's constant hustling of pot, only one thing that might be called eventful happened to him in those two years. At least it was inwardly eventful. It was also astonishing. His exposure to religion and churches had never been more than superficial. Once in a while in seizures of piety that lasted a few weeks his mother had used to drag him, and anybody else she could manage, to services, including both Sunday night and Wednesday prayer meeting, at the High Hope Primitive Baptist Church. Otherwise, except for her frequent pious mouthings, he was accustomed to hearing God's name mainly in the oaths of his father and brothers. As the remote cause of outstandingly good or bad things that happened He would come to Wendell's mind, but at other times Wendell thought little enough about the deity. Nor had he been thinking about Him when, just a few months before his eighteenth birthday, he was most alarmingly stricken. *Why* it happened remained mysterious but the vividness of the recollection did not go out of his mind.

It was a night revival meeting, in a tent, like a thousand others he had seen in and around Bison Springs. In passing he stopped because he had nothing else to do and because he thought that just maybe he might be able, when the meeting broke up, to scout out a buyer for his wares.

Wendell was not even inside the tent. Where he stood, in a thin rank of uncommitted auditors like himself, was just beyond the perimeter of bright light from the hanging bulbs inside and he supposed that the preacher even if he were to try would be able to see his face as a shadow only. Besides this the preacher was at full tilt, pacing hugely—he was bigger than big—from side to side of the tent and waving his Bible and pleading with or threatening the sheep seated in rows on the chairs. It was routine stuff. The devil and the pit of hell were in it, and Jesus' love and the wages of sin. Wendell did notice when *dope* got into it but this in recent years had also become routine. He remembered the big yawn he finally gave. Whether or not his yawn was the reason, all of a sudden things were not routine any longer.

Everything had stopped. The preacher, like a tower, was just standing there in the middle of the most alarming silence Wendell had ever experienced, an alarm that came from his certainty that the preacher was not only looking at him but seeing his face as plainly as if it had been focused in the sun's fiercest beam. There was no escape. All, everything that Wendell knew about himself, and more, much more that he did not know, was here as hideously bared as if hell had suddenly been laid open. That glare from the preacher's eyes was on him like a seizure making impossible the least movement of Wendell's body.

The voice resounded. The Bible, uplifted in the powerful hand, made two slow arcs above the preacher's head, and sank, and all of a sudden Wendell found that he could move again. He did it slowly, inching backward, lest he recall that glare to the preacher's face. Reaching a point where the dark could not but hide him, he turned and fled.

It was the most unaccountable thing in the world and the effects of it dogged him for weeks. The worst part was the first few days. He could not sleep and he lay on his cot in the night expecting that at any moment something, like maybe a hand as big as himself, would seize him. Instead of sleep he fell into swoons that were a sort of downward hurtling and from which he would wake in panic and leave his bed. In daytime he could not shed the impression that somebody was following him. He was always turning abruptly around, for nothing.

For nothing, that is, except on one occasion. This time there was somebody and it was, of all human beings, that preacher. Not that he was following Wendell, he was only standing there on the street corner that Wendell had just now walked blindly past. Nor was he looking at Wendell. Wendell was the one who was looking, staring, amazed now at the size of the man. Though slight of build, Wendell was not a small person. But looking at the man even from a distance of ten paces he felt himself a dwarf or infant child, a creature that the man might reach out and lay hold of and without inconvenience swallow down. Tiny Bubba, too small to resist.

The enormous head did turn and look at him. And recognize him too, he thought, because he saw in the eyes, a mottled yellow brown, intentness quickly contract itself to a point. Tiny Bubba, dwindling, about to be swallowed. And afterwards, after the preacher's eyes had finished with him and he was crossing the street, he felt in an eerie way as though this had happened—his essence drawn in through those eyes and forever stored away in the huge recording mind.

Those were difficult weeks. He spent them not only in fear and trembling but also in the fanatical practice of everything he thought to be a virtue. After the first few days—he delayed because he kept imagining that the mere touch might bring some terror to pass—he fetched a Bible lying dustily on a bottom shelf in his sister's living room and set himself to read it from cover to cover. He was soon skipping, and it seemed for a while, in his half-dark closet of a room, that some power kept guiding his eye to yet another withering display of God's wrath toward sinners. Outer darkness, everlasting fire: these were the kinds of phrases that made his guts contract. But he plugged on and in subsequent days found that there were comforting parts that made the reading tolerable. These even made it possible for him, on the second Sunday, to risk attending a church. This happened twice, on successive Sundays. After that, because he was cured, he never went again.

But that interlude left his equanimity disturbed for a considerable time. He had had no idea of himself as vulnerable to childish affliction like that and he wondered what might have happened if that oversized God-crazy preacher had not folded his tent and stolen away before Wendell made his choice of a church to go to: it could have been a fate worse than death. Instead, as it seemed to him, he was maybe saved by his own perfectly blind choice. He barely knew one church from another and he happened to strike on one in Bison Springs where a youthful preacher with cheeks like ripe peaches spoke soft enlightened words. His message as such meant nothing to Wendell but it cooled his fevered brow and helped to wash out of his mind the dark affliction that had closed on it. From his heart he thanked the young preacher for that. He only hoped that the first preacher would be as forgettable as this one. Wendell hated the thought of that son of a bitch.

Anyway his health had come back and he returned to his suspended activities with a certain addition of zeal. But this only after a slightly disconcerting conference with Cat Bird, who had been inconvenienced by Wendell's temporary apostasy. "You done mess us up, Wen'll," he said. "Big Man don't like that."

Wendell had caught him in the alley in back of the pool hall. Cat stood there, springy on his feet, darting glances back and forth from Wendell's face to the billiard ball rolling between the quick thin juggler's fingers of his black right hand. His name, or nickname, fitted him uncommonly well. He had the kind of abrasive voice that that particular bird has got and, like that or any other bird, the habit of almost constant hair-trigger movements. Especially in the face he was never quite still, and people were always unsure as to when, if at all, Cat was looking directly at them. This made people feel a little off-balance with him and sometimes, unless they considered those fragile arms and legs, vaguely threatened. Not that his demeanor was in any way threatening. In fact it was nearly always good humored and on those rare occasions when his green eyes flicked coldly across a person's face, that person was much more likely to respond by merely wondering what he meant.

"I've been feeling bad," Wendell said. "I just wasn't up to it."

"Don't lay out no more. That what the Big Man say . . . not me."

"He did, huh?" Wendell said, not quite containing a small surge of defiance. "Big Man. Who is he anyway? You never have told me."

This was one of those moments when, visible in light from the back door of the pool hall where the balls clicked, Cat's cold glance crossed Wendell's face. His expression changed and he looked up at the sky. "He name writ in the stars. He move on the wind like . . ."

"Cut the crap. Who is he?"

"He come like the lightning fall from the sky . . ."

"Shit! Have you got something for me or not?"

"Be in the parking lot one hour from now."

He watched Cat go springing off down the alley and he wondered again, just as he had wondered about everything else connected with Cat, where he lived and where he had come from. Bird, if that was his name, was not the name of any family, black or white, that Wendell had ever heard of in the county and he supposed that Cat must have come here from some place far off. He had that kind of an air about him, not like a local black man. He held a job lifting and cleaning up at Casey's Feed and Seed but he did not seem to have a home, not around Bison Springs. If he had any friends Wendell had never seen them. It was a waste of time to ask him personal questions because if one did he would be treated to some such rhapsodic foolishness as Wendell had got when he asked him who the Big Man was. This was the question to which Wendell most wanted an answer. It was to be a long time before he found out.

Anyway Cat Bird and everything connected with him had finally begun to make Wendell uneasy somehow, even while he went about hustling with a good deal of zest. When the time came for him to go off to college he was almost as glad to be getting rid of Cat as of anything else around Bison Springs. He had come to the notion that in a way he could not fathom, something here was getting a hold on him.

V

The college to which Wendell's scholarship was the key was a hundred miles away in the sizable town of Dukesboro. (It was a year before he began to refer it as Kooksboro). The college itself, Goodwin College, was a fairly provincial place but Wendell was not able to see this at the time. For all the difference in his mind it might have been Oxford or the Sorbonne. College. Not only had nobody in any way kin to him ever attended a college; not one, he was certain, had ever even thought about the possibility. Yet here he was, in a condition so wide-eyed that it was weeks before he could get a sound night's sleep.

The campus had eleven different buildings besides the central one with a tower and a clock that chimed the hours, all set down in one great green lawn that a crew with riding mowers was always clipping. There was shade of elms and water oaks and behind the central building a large mall of different-colored bricks where the students gathered. For the first few weeks, between classes, he would sit on the little wall at the end of it and watch the students come and go or gathered chattering or horseplaying. Their casualness was astonishing: when later he read the phrase *at ease in Zion* he had words to express what he felt then. All of them, but especially the girls in their turned-outness, their poise, were a breed apart from the people he had known and he sat thinking that he never would become one of them. In essence he was right.

There were, as Wendell finally recognized, some students who had come from origins nearly as redneck as his own, but

35

somehow they managed what he was neither able nor willing to do: suppress or obscure in their own minds the sense of this identity. Not that he proclaimed it. The time came when he had mastered a persona not distinguishable from those of his more polished classmates. But he knew it for what it was, an appearance, and that underneath was the secret Wendell as intact as on that first day when he had set his awed gaze on Kooksboro and its shining college.

There was strength in a secret like this, a certain feeling of invulnerability. Together with a conviction of mental superiority that his performance as a student confirmed in him, it fed the germ of disdain or contempt for everybody around him. Not only for those around him, though: he did not experience any belated birth of loyalty toward his own kind. He was simply himself, alone. And the direction in which his interests as a student took him was in its way an expression of this fact.

English literature, of all things, was what he chose for his major. His old habit of reading had something to do with this decision but the greater reason was his determination to define himself with as wide a margin as possible between him and the rest, including especially the sorry lot of folks he had derived from. If he was a redneck he was his own kind of redneck and this choice was a sort of declaration of the fact. The choice was all the more deliberate in that its disadvantages were clear to him. What about the world out there where he intended to go? Did he want to be another scruffy teacher of English majors yet to come? He stifled such questions with the thought that a man should follow where his talents led.

His talents were real, though, and he was never very far from the top of his class. In his third year he conceived the idea that he was a writer and the fact that some of his poems and stories got printed in the student literary magazine confirmed him in this idea of himself. Here was his purpose, this was what he would take into the world. In time he would, after he had prepared himself and got his material together. He did not write very much but he hung on tight to the idea. He was a writer. It was no wonder, then, that he stood always apart, alone, the secretly laughing observer of his fellow students at their antics—his characters. He fitted the pattern. This together with his literary successes got him finally a small reputation on campus, which in turn strengthened his hold on this idea of himself. Becoming at last a habit it permitted him to justify behavior that otherwise would not have borne much scrutiny.

No doubt Wendell's reputation was a factor in his professors' estimate of his abilities. In any case in his senior year some of them urged graduate school upon him, promising strong letters in his behalf and the riches (spiritual) accruing to lives whose ministry was the rescue of souls from darkness. The graduate school to which they referred was that at the state university, which was not twenty-five miles from Bison Springs and which anyway was not for Wendell a place of high romance. His soul yawned at the prospect. And yet he went. Where else was he to go? Not yet prepared to practice his vocation he could not do better, he told himself, than spend another year or two with books.

Wendell left Dukesboro for Drayton without regret. He had made no friends and he brought with him only the most residual memories of the several girls who had fallen to the seductions of his prestige as a writer. At the state university, though, where he was once again among strangers and where his former prestige had not accompanied him he began, unexpectedly, to feel a need for some kind of human relationships. He made an effort, disguising himself with smiles and friendly words. It did not work, not really. All it ever achieved was an invitation now and then to one of those bashes in somebody's too-small apartment where they drank whiskey and smoked pot and, when they were not too stoned, discoursed in exotic terms about Nietzsche and the postmodern spirit.

"If you reflect on it . . . really reflect . . . what do you mean by *meaning?*" This sort of thing from the fat lips of such a one as Calvin Sims, who from behind rimless lenses as thick as plate glass probably could not see one feature of the rapt faces watching him through the smoke.

"Therefore, what?" This voice, throaty, was Lucy Singer's, urging another display of that steel-trap mind.

Wendell forced himself to participate, though more and more at subsequent gatherings he had trouble talking with his tongue in his cheek. He stopped trying and along in the winter deprived them of his company as well as his wisdom. Not, however, before he had established one intimacy with a fellow student—a girl named Milly Hollander.

The affair was of short duration and Wendell remembered it best for the discomfort it generated. Once again the spark had derived from his literary efforts, in this case a poem that reminded Milly of Yeats in his early period and set her all atingle. Almost every day for two or three weeks they thrashed around in the bed in her grubby apartment, savoring the best of life. Then the discomfort started. She had very large dark eyes that could get darker and nipples that were just about as vivid on her white breasts as her eyes were in her face. It was as though she was accusing him with both pairs of organs.

"You said you wanted sex," Wendell would say to her, putting on his clothes. "Looks like you ought to be satisfied."

"You could at least . . ." She did not finish.

"What? I've done everything I could."

She would leave it at this, or something like this, and Wendell would go on dressing under the weight of a gaze that was wounded as well as accusing. To shed his small discomfort he would look out the window and over the tree and rooftops to where he could see the clockface in the tower of Ridley Hall. Then he was likely to feel vexation coming on and after that, once he was outside, a small grin starting to spread his lips. He was recalling what he thought he had discovered about her: that behind it all she was nothing but a rich girl come here slumming. So it was maybe true that people got what they asked for in the world. Wendell, however, soon got something he had not asked for, the cold shoulder. By then he did not care much.

VI

Wendell had two reasons for being glad, in fact exultant, when the quarter came to an end. One of course was release from the tedium, not to say burning vexation, of his days at the university, where he continued mindlessly to hang on as if that job had been the one and only lifeline possible for him. His other reason was that now he was going to have the house all to himself. Rathbone, a jubilant Rathbone, had been awarded a research grant that would enable him to go to London for the summer. A book, a book on guess who, would come of it, he announced, gazing rapturously up through the cloud of pot smoke he had just then exhaled. He would go unaccompanied. But Alice, obviously miffed, would be absent also, gone in pursuit of interests of her own which were to be satisfied at a kind of summer camp for the enlightened. Contented if not quite golden hours seemed a sure prospect for Wendell.

But his expectations were not fulfilled, not after the first day or two. In that brief interval he kept himself frenetically busy cleaning up the house, the kitchen first and then the whole place room by room, omitting only that room sacred to the amorous flame supposed to exist between the hare-brained masters of the house. This of course was the worst room of all and Wendell did enter it and stand for a time before he changed his mind. His intrusion would have been resented. For another thing the condition of that room seemed irremediable except maybe by a good fire. Garments and soiled bedclothes stuffed in corners, spills on the rug and dresser top, even a vaguely pungent smell that put him in mind of pot and sexual hijinks.

There was one object, though, that caught and held his eye for a minute and left him surprised in a way that his close-up view of the room's chaos had not. It was a photograph, on the dresser, of a sweet-faced old lady. Rathbone actually had a mother, one who would actually write *To my beloved Tug* on a picture that he would actually keep displayed in a place of prominence. For a minute or two these were real facts for Wendell. Once outside the room, however, and afterwards when he thought about the picture at all he remembered it as if it had been a fiction he himself had cooked up in one of his creative efforts.

The end of Wendell's housecleaning days also brought him to the end of his contentment. It did more than this. Beginning that same night after he had eaten supper and washed up and stood admiring the perfection of the cleanliness he had wrought he fell into a state of mind unlike any he could remember experiencing. It was not a thing of the moment. It pursued him into sleep and almost without remission through the next day and the days that followed. At first he thought the cause was simply the stillness of the house, a stillness unlike the accustomed hush that fell when the voices stopped. He tried the TV, dragging it out of its corner. He tried the radio, playing it softly in his room while he, pencil in hand, sat staring at the dead white page before him. He was a young man accustomed all his life to being by himself, with only himself for company. What had happened? Nothing that he could finger, and yet, suddenly, it was as if the old companion self had absconded on him, leaving silence within him as well as without. He was the stillest thing in the house, the center of all the stillness, as powerless as any ghost to enter the world of sound.

His attempts at remedy were walks in the hot streets and work in the garden and at night the pot that Rathbone kept well hidden under the chicken coop out back. None of these helped much, and the pot, when he made his way back from those slow journeys into no special place, only made the stillness sing louder than ever. On the fifth day he unearthed Rathbone's car keys in the litter of a drawer, and drove. He drove to Drayton, quiet without the students in town, and then, for no identifiable reason, headed north to the interstate and on toward Atlanta a hundred miles away.

He thought he had in mind that this trip would be a first step, or at least a foot in the door, into the great world. He stayed two nights. His room was in a grungy hotel at the edge of the downtown section and from there he walked, and walked, street after street, pausing like any yokel to stare up at the topless towers and into store windows and faces that unseeingly passed him by. He walked at night too, dangerously he was sure, down streets that along toward twelve o'clock were half-lit canyons deserted except for him.

On the second night he encountered a bum. Or rather, he came up in the bum's tracks and, slowing his steps to match the creeping pace, followed him for a couple of blocks. The bum turned into an alley and when Wendell passed it the bum was just steps beyond the corner crouched against the wall. He seemed to be looking at Wendell but in that light he was faceless. Probably Wendell only imagined that the bum made some gesture as of greeting and he wondered what the bum would have said his name was, assuming he could remember it. When Wendell left the next day he had not checked on a single one of the help wanted ads in the newspapers he had bought.

So he drove back but not straight back. He went out of his way to pass through Bison Springs, where he got no glimpse of a face he recognized, and take Highway 17 over to Turnbull. About three miles from Turnbull he slowed down. The country there was rolling pasture and cotton land and a person could see a long way before he came to it the stark redbrick structure that was the state Home For The Infirm. He wanted time to think some more and when he came to the turnoff where the drive mounted up to the parking lot he had let the car drift almost to a stop. He did stop, on the highway shoulder, and sat there for a while. In the end he got back on the pavement and drove on to Turnbull. For what was the sense in it, now or ever—to pay a visit he did not want to pay, to a man who would not know the difference in either case? That slate was five years clean. Now it would stay this way.

Although Wendell had known quite well that the house would be no less empty when he got back, he found himself, even as he opened the kitchen door, with an ear already cocked for sound, a footfall maybe or a muted voice from up-stairs. In fact he glanced around the kitchen for signs of new disorder. None, nothing changed, or course. He walked with loud steps through the living room to the hall and up the dim staircase and back to his bedroom. There, gazing out through the rear window, he could hear the stillness sealing his ears again. But something focused his gaze all of a sudden.

It was midafternoon and hot, an hour when even the most zealous of gardeners sought the shade. Yet there she was, Miss Tricia, in the blistering white sunlight, bonneted, with hoe in hand, stroking away at evil weeds between her rows of corn. Some whole minutes passed while from his silent window he watched and watched her move on down the row until, at the end, she stopped and, lifting a shirt-sleeved arm, drew it across her forehead under her bonnet. She looked up then, and though it was impossible to tell from this distance he thought she looked directly at his window. In any case she got a response. He not only turned from the window, he went downstairs and straight on out to the gap in the hedge back there. This time it was he who spoke to her from the gap.

Wendell had thought only to talk for a few minutes and hear a voice, even hers, answer him back: that was all. Evidently this was not enough, though, or he would have found a way to refuse the invitation that in a matter of minutes she was pressing on him. "We can have some iced tea and we can have that talk. You know, I almost think you've been avoiding me," she said with comic woefulness. The glare of afternoon was not so kind to her face as that twilight hour had been, and under the too-large man's shirt she wore even those fetching amplitudes he had noted that evening seemed more like bulges. She was still all right, though. He went along.

He was not sorry. For one thing it was a pleasant house, not grand exactly but distinctive with an air of old Confederate times carefully preserved—the kind of house, he reflected, into which no Corbin before him could ever have been invited. This in fact was one of the considerations that pleased him about his decision. A Corbin in the house, a disguised Corbin conducted from room to room amid the lady's bright chatter about this old piece of furniture and that and how the floorboards and the staircase in the big front hall had been restored and how the Yankees had quartered here and made the place a wreck before they left. He nodded, mouthing his admiration or clucking his dismay at the Yankees' barbarous conduct. Smiling too, sometimes—a genuine Corbin smile that she took for pleasure in what she showed him.

Their tour lasted more minutes than he would have chosen to give it but near the end, in the tall living room full of spidery chairs and three-legged tables and one massive polished cabinet, a small incident occurred. It came of that smile on his face. Among several gilt-framed portraits on the walls, there was one of a young, handsome, and rather haughty-seeming woman and though he was not exactly concentrating on it Tricia clearly thought he was. Her silence was what got Wendell's attention. She wore an expression he had not seen until now. Tricia had full lips but in this moment, pressed tight together, they did not appear so, and the expression produced in her face could only be described as a scowl. This raised a question mark in Wendell's mind but also the thought that he rather liked her expression: it put something where he had not seen anything much before.

What she said then amused him. "My mother-in-law. When she was young." She said it in a subdued voice that told the old story with a special, biting intensity.

Tricia quickly brightened again and in the spacious well-scrubbed kitchen sat him down at a table covered with a red oilcloth. A breeze came in from the shaded back gallery outside the door and Wendell reflected that if he was in for a conversational ordeal at least he would be permitted to suffer it in pleasant surroundings.

In fact the ordeal was soon under way, even while Tricia was still at the counter beside the big yellow refrigerator preparing two huge glasses of tea topped with mint. There was nothing like iced tea, she said. But this was an interruption merely bracketed in a monologue already at full current, whose subject, unhappily, was Nietzsche once again. Wendell was surprised. That evening in the garden he had supposed that this affair of hers could not possibly amount to more than a one- or two-night stand. Yet here she was, weeks later, still befuddling herself with the oracles of that old vapor-wit Zarathustra. Could there be, he wondered, anything serious inside this little brain? It was hard to imagine.

It was even harder when, presenting him with the tea, she sat down at the other side of the table, where he could look into her face. Her eyes, innocently blue, reflected the brightness of the voice in which she chattered on about ideas as congenial as so many loaded bombs to the only world she knew anything about. Except that in her hands the bombs were not loaded, they were toys, and the brief smiles that kept stretching her mouth seemed to tell him that she was even a trifle embarrassed to be playing with them at her age. She did not falter, though.

Of course there were questions for Wendell, the intellectual, to which he bumbled out answers that impressed her. Fortunately there were other intervals, asides of a domestic kind that by contrast were small mercies to his harried wits. It almost seemed interesting to learn that her husband's name was Joe and that he traveled for a large hardware manufacturer in Birmingham and that he was at home a great deal less than she had a right to expect. Wendell learned to his surprise that there was a son aged sixteen who was *never* at home, who went away to school and away to other places in the summer.

A few additional facts got in. She was not a local girl but from another small town, Halesboro, that Wendell had never heard of. He was also informed that she, though not Joe, was a college graduate, of a college named Morton that he thought he had maybe heard of. But she had only majored in home economics, she said, with a smile of self-deprecation that lasted a second or two. Here, in this pause, was one more instance when, hoping to keep her out of Zarathustra's tracks, he opened his mouth too late. The moment was too brief for his benumbed reflexes.

"You read it, you know, and you can't help but think things," she said. "About yourself, I mean." The innocent blue eyes, not yet beginning to fade, were wide open looking at him. He observed her hand on the tea glass—tapered fingers, rather nice. Rather nice too was the triangle of sun-tinted flesh where the outsized man's shirt lay parted down from her throat. She did have assets capable of engaging intelligent interest.

"Like being honest," she went on, "about all the things you're supposed to believe in that maybe you don't really. And not being creative, so you're just kind of stuck in the mud. Like an old hog or something. And not ever being free because you just go on acting like you still think what everybody always told you to. Of course I never could be any *hero*," she said, with that little stretch of her mouth. "I couldn't even be a *bridge* to the Ubermensch, like he talks about. I'd always be worried about what people were thinking about me. Besides, I never could believe there's not really a God. Could you?"

Focusing his eyes Wendell said, a bit belatedly, "I'm not sure."

"How could there by any world, then, if people just made Him up?"

Wendell shook his head over this one.

"He believes it, though. I remember a sentence I've got underlined in my book. 'It was suffering and incapacity that created all Afterworlds.'" She paused, looking at Wendell as if he had said it and ought to be willing to defend it. He refused, though with a deeply thoughtful expression, and she went on, "I've thought and thought about that. I was thinking . . ."

Wendell was thinking too but his thought was about the modern craze to start any and everybody *thinking*. With minds like hers caught up in unequal struggle this now-headlong rage for pot and drugs was hardly a wonder. Not that there was any real struggle here. It was more of a side-show, a drama cooked up to fill her empty hours. And also, surely, to impress—Wendell in the present case. Trying another diversion he broke in, "What does your husband think about all this?"

This did stop her, made her blink. "Joe?" she said as if she was not sure who Wendell was talking about. "Oh he wouldn't understand it. He would think it was all crazy. We never . . ."

Something had happened. Wendell believed for a moment that she had had a really striking thought, or else a stab of pain somewhere. Her eyes had left him and now were trained on the hall door off to her right. Glancing he did not see anything through the door but when he looked back her fixed posture had not changed. When it did and she looked at him again he knew there was something out there. Joe, maybe, come home unexpectedly—a jealous Joe? Her expression suggested as much and so did her manner, her subdued voice when she tried to get back on Zarathustra. Before she gave it up completely and fell silent he could hear that somebody was indeed approaching. It turned out to be a white-haired old woman with a cane.

"My mother-in-law," Tricia murmured and they both sat watching the old woman limp painfully in through the door.

Wendell was never trained to stand up when a woman came into the room and certainly there was nothing in his more recent experience to change his habits. This time, though, he had made a mistake. He had been dismissed before in his life but never like this, in quite such a silence, in a gaze as coldly surgical as this old woman's was. Near the end of Tricia's strained introduction he tried to mend things, popping out of his chair. It was too late and he had the feeling that her scrutiny had cut even deeper into him than he at first thought. His courteous enough "Glad to know you, Mrs. Harker" elicited nothing except "Please sit down, young man," spoken in a perfectly flat voice. Wendell did sit down, immediately, thinking only then, with surprise at himself, What the hell do I care what she thinks?

His name, he believed, was part of the reason for his discomfort. When Tricia had said, "This is Wendell Corbin, Mother," something at the back of his mind took hold and then, as if in full view of the old woman's surgical eye, bloomed up. It was an exposure like nakedness almost, shameful. Nor did it help much when in the next breath Tricia lightsomely explained that he was a stranger to these parts, a graduate student in English, from Georgia. It was only after he had sat down and was no longer an object of the old woman's scrutiny that his anger surged up. Ridiculous. But it was a while before he could fully recover his spirit of ironic detachment.

Meanwhile as a sort of participant he witnessed the exercise of Mother's sway over poor little Tricia. She was saying in a voice nearly as flat as before, "I hope you didn't forget my medicine, Patricia."

"Oh I'm sorry, Mother. It's out in the car, I'll get it right now." Preparing to rise Tricia already had her hands on the table, but Mother's voice stopped her.

"No. I can wait until your friend leaves." Though again directed Wendell's way for a second, her gaze did not seem to include him among the things she saw: it was more as if she had looked at an empty chair.

"I can get . . ." But Tricia was stopped again.

"No, I'll wait. Finish your conversation."

But Wendell was not about to leave now, not on this bullying note, even if he did feel that he had better avoid Tricia's eyes. Among other things, he wanted to see whether the old girl would keep on standing there for as long as he chose to extend his visit. So he tried a gambit, a question to Tricia about Joe and his work. The answer came in a rather strained voice that because his attention was on Mother he just did hear.

Mother's attention was on him also, he was pleased to note, feeling himself become visible again. She was standing like a big old bird near the end of the table, both hands on the knob of the cane, bent a little toward a point between Tricia and him. He realized that she would have been quite tall if she had stood up straight and he had a fleeting thought about the Lady Madeline of Usher—fleeting because the image was not too apt. The Lady Madeline surely had not possessed this kind of iron intolerant jaw or the still-vigorous though white hair that proclaimed her at least not so ancient as she had appeared at first. It was mainly the posture, the arthritis or whatever, that fooled one about her great age.

" . . . and it's really a very big company, one of the biggest," Tricia was saying to him, with occasional oblique glances up at Mother. "Joe's very good at his job, he's a born . . ." She broke off. "Mother, I'd better go get . . ."

"No, I'll wait over here," Mother said, turning laboriously and starting her trek across the kitchen to a stool near the sink in back of Tricia. "I like to hear people talk," she added.

Tricia stared at the wall behind Wendell. Mother completed her small journey and cautiously settled herself on the stool. Seated she held the knobbed cane like a weapon with both hands at her knees. "Go on with your conversation," she said. "I thought perhaps you were taking about 'Nitch' before I came in."

Tricia's face did not change. "Excuse me, Mother, I didn't understand you."

"I suppose it must be 'Nietzsche.' I hope you don't mind that I peeped into your book a little, Patricia."

Tricia kept on staring at the wall.

"In my opinion it's a book full of wicked foolishness. But I'm an old woman."

Poor Tricia clearly thought an answer was called for. She looked at Wendell, for help, but he had none to give. Anyway he was beginning to enjoy the situation. A silent minute passed, in which, seemingly for the first time, he heard the ticking of a clock in the adjacent dining room.

"Well, so be it," Mother said. She was gazing straight off through space, through the back window maybe at the trees beyond the gallery. After another pause she said, "And your name, young man, is Corbin?"

Tricia glanced at him. "Wendell Corbin, Mother."

"There used to be some Corbins over around Bison Springs. Quite a lot of them, as I remember."

"Wendell is from Georgia. He's a graduate student at the university." Tricia was looking past him and did not, Wendell hoped, notice the way his face had stiffened.

"I'm glad of that," Mother said. "A feckless lot." She drew a breath. "But I expect that by now they are all selling automobiles or something. Like that awful Jason Farrow. Everybody's selling something nowadays. Even my Joe."

Despite his anger Wendell observed that he was not the only one who had stiffened. Tricia's expression, except for its greater intensity, was the one she had worn in front of the portrait in the living room. All of a sudden his anger was gone, or forgotten if not gone. He was waiting to see, watching Tricia's face, waiting for Mother's voice again. Tricia's voice came first.

"Mr. Farrow was awfully good to Joe when he worked there."

Mother must have heard this but she gave no sign. Gazing into space she said, "That's the way it is now. Look at this county. Or any other one. It isn't a question anymore of the bottom rail's being on top, the rails are all the same. I'd like to think this state of things will go away, but of course it won't. I look out a window sometimes and see that hairy fellow next door. Living in Hubert Dowlin's old house. There never was a better man than Hubert Dowlin." She was still for a second. "But this fellow. There was a day when they would have taken that man and sheared him like a sheep."

"That's Professor Rathbone. From the university. He's a renowned scholar," Tricia said, her eyes still fastened on the wall. The scowl had if anything tightened on her face and her flat tone was a near match for the old woman's. Maybe, just maybe, Wendell thought again, there might be a core of something in her.

"University," Mother said without any change of voice. "There used to be a university. Where gentlemen taught gentlemen the things they ought to know. In the days before *football*. And drugs. Those terrible drugs."

The *gentlemen* may have been aimed at Wendell but the drugs was not, he decided. Whatever, he was too caught up in the little drama to feel any bite in her words. He was waiting on Tricia now, pulling for her.

"Wendell is with the university, Mother."

Here it was again, the show of spunk.

"Yes. You told me." Mother was still for a moment. "Even the children," she said. "Like the Farnsworth boy, that died of drugs two weeks ago." Her head gave a tremulous movement. "For a long time there I had almost stopped believing in the devil. I've come back to it. I don't know how else to explain what's happened." In a voice suddenly tired and irritable she said, "I must have my medicine now."

Tricia unscrewed her face and looked at him. She meant Go, and when she stood up, Wendell was left without any choice. He stood up too, with a muted farewell to the tired eyes watching him from across the kitchen. But Tricia had still another small display of guts in store for him. Right there in the full gaze of the old dragon she said in a cheery voice, "You'll come again soon, won't you?"

Wendell said he would, or something, and was about to be disappointed in her when, prefaced by a defiant blink of her eyes, Tricia stood up and said, "By the way, you can walk me to the garage."

VII

A domestic comedy starring Tricia. Wendell conceived the idea, in a bolt of inspiration, on the night that followed their session in her kitchen, and before he went to bed he had actually written the opening sentences of this promising novel. His literary production consisted mostly of just such beginnings but in this case he continued to feel that he really had his hands on something. A week went by and though he never worked except by spurts he was still at it, still making plans. For once he could not plead a lack of spare time. He had too much time and he spent some of it puttering in his garden. But much more to his purpose were the hours he spent in colloquy with his collaborator.

Collaborator was not actually the right word because Tricia was not conscious of making any contribution. This was Wendell's design, to trick her into helps and hints which she gave with increasing openness as their friendship matured. In fact, once the ice was really broken, his purpose required practically no tricking at all. Up to a point, at least, she wanted to reveal herself. She wanted to talk about Nietzsche and such rare matters but she wanted equally to talk about herself and about Joe and about the whole town of Turnbull. Most of all, however, she wanted to talk about Mother, a name that issued from between lips always ever so slightly tensed. Wendell became almost her confessor, full of acute if often designing advice. He was aware of stealing up on her soul through the back door but he assuaged his small discomfort with the thought that all would come out in disguise, transfigured in his novel.

All of their meetings for a while were confined to that gap in the hedge between the gardens and despite the privacy back there were always, on her part, a little strained. Tongues might wag, she said, and would add, in her tone of coy self-denigration, that she was not any Nietzschean hero. Anyway little by little he got the general picture of her life.

Her father was a small—very small, Wendell gathered—grocer in Halesboro whose character was typified by the fact that he forebade or tried to forbid his three daughters to participate in any social activities not connected with the church. Tricia was the defiant one and somehow withstood, or evaded, the storm of his rage that never relented throughout her career as a cheerleader at the high school. She even sneaked out on dates with some of the wilder boys in hot-rods, risking weeks of confinement and family prayers for her soul. The cheerleading paid off, though. Along with good grades it helped to get her to not-very-distant Morton College, where, also over her father's protest, she found her independence, returning home only for brief visits even during the summer. Her two sisters got married shortly after graduating from high school and she lost touch with them. After Tricia herself got married she practically lost touch with her parents.

At Morton was where she met Joe and immediately after graduating married him, eloped with him. He had not been passing at the state university and had transferred down there and once they were married he dropped out of college for good. The long delay before they came to live at Joe's home in Turnbull was easy to understand: the fact of the elopement reflected their uneasiness about the kind of welcome they might expect. But things were hard for them and after about a year, in spite of the uncertain music to be faced, they accepted the invitation extended by Mother and Father both.

However muffled in courtesy discord was there from the start, and maybe if Father, the Judge, had not died six months later their residence in his home would not have become permanent. Tricia was a large disappointment to Joe's parents and she got and kept the impression that they at least partly blamed her for Joe's inherent shortcomings. The family name and standards were important to both of them. The father stood third in a line of respected judges and Mother, from a prominent though much diminished plantation family, had even more than her husband expectations for her son. But how was it Tricia's fault that Joe was content, at least for five years, to go on selling automobiles at what was then Mr. Henry's small Ford agency in town? In fact it had not contented Tricia. She was, herself, the one who, awhile after Jason Farrow bought the agency, had most urged Joe to take the job with the hardware manufacturer in Birmingham.

But the discord between Tricia and the soon-widowed mother was by no means only on account of Joe. What Tricia had to live with—had always had to live with, she declared—was the old woman's never-quite-buried disdain. The cause at bottom was Tricia's family, because they were not Anybody, and out of this the old woman had spun all her barely suppressed grievances against Tricia, just for being Tricia. "And different from *her*," Tricia said with feeling, "because she's such an *aristocrat*."

But Wendell's clearest impression so far of her relationship with Mother came two weeks after his first visit, when Tricia invited him into the house again. The act had nothing of the heroic about it. Mother was absent, hauled off by son Joe to the doctor up at Drayton, and the route into the house by the back door was invisible to any eyes not stationed in one of the high windows on Wendell's side of the hedge.

In the assured privacy of her kitchen, where the breeze and now and then a birdsong came in through the open door and mote-filled rays of sunlight cast patterns on the red floor tiles, Tricia came closer than ever before to really parting the curtain. Wendell learned, without even probing, details about Joe, who had been a rather shadowy figure in his mind. Things were less than well between Tricia and him, though she did not say this in so many words. In fact she made an effort, if a slightly hypocritical one, to hide it behind a smile of comic resignation. "I've gotten almost used to being a nurse," she said. "For *his* sake, he's so devoted to her. He gets so upset when I complain, poor thing." The smile came here, tense at the corners.

"Maybe you ought to put your foot down," Wendell said. This was not strong enough and he added, "I sure would. I'd make a big scene out of it."

"She'd just get meaner than ever. And Joe would sulk for weeks."

"Let them, then. I would." He thought that in fact this was sound advice.

"She can be so awful . . . " Tricia settled for *ugly*, clearly rejecting a stronger word. She lowered her face but he could see the set of her lips. "And Joe just . . . " She never did finish. Her fingers revolved the glass of tea on the table.

"It looks to me like he's got it coming. At least he could spend some time at home, couldn't he?"

"They're always sending him places. Then he has meetings and things. . . . It's not much better when he's here, anyway." She said this last in a faint voice, her attention apparently elsewhere. When she spoke again her voice had tightened.

"She could perfectly well do it herself, other people give themselves diabetes shots. Not her, *I* have to do it. She's too *delicate*. She likes to make me wait on her, like I was a servant. Then she thinks I stick her in the same place on purpose. I don't but I'm glad when it happens."

"Good for you," Wendell said.

"She's got a kind of look I can always read. It comes right down her nose. It means I'm little Miss Nobody Tricia. She thinks everybody's low class but her. Except maybe Joe. I think she's kind of glad when he goes away, so he won't be with me." She ended by looking straight at Wendell, not scowling exactly, just stiff in the face. He thought he had never really noticed before how blue her eyes were.

"Joe's just a mama's boy. . . . When he's not being somebody else's *boy*."

"I think it's time to put your foot down, hard," Wendell said, trying to imagine it. Less weightily he said, "Be a hero, like you've been reading about in Nietzsche."

She looked embarrassed, dropped her gaze. If in fact Wendell was making fun of her he had not intended to let it show. "I wasn't laughing at you, I'm serious. You're putting up with way too much."

Whether this was helpful or not, a pause followed in which neither of them was able to say anything. He thought that maybe her embarrassment was not because of his remark but because in her anger she had spilled more than a proper housewife should. To rescue the situation he made a request. He had been wanting to see the house again, with a writer's eye this time, and here was an occasion.

She led him, though with little to say this trip, once more through the dining room and the living room and on between the staircase and the big front doors to the parlor across the hall. Without his asking she even opened the door to the bedroom that was hers and Joe's across the hall from the kitchen. Opposite the door was a tester bed with its blue coverlet drawn tight. For the few seconds before they turned away the two of them stood silently looking in. This was a moment that Wendell later recalled with a surge of his pulse, remembering the ripe look of her body under the jeans and the man's shirt she wore.

Another moment he was to recall occurred upstairs, where he had not expected to be invited. At the foot of the staircase, looking up the stairwell to the sunlit hall above, she made the unnecessary statement that there were rooms up there too. With nothing more said she led him up.

There were four rooms, three bedrooms and one used for storage, and a bathroom at the rear of the hall. Though Tricia did not say so or indeed say anything, clearly the back room on the right belonged to Mother. Through the doorway Wendell could see medicine bottles on a table next to the brass bed—one of the bottles overturned, with capsules spilling out—and garments lying over the back of a rocker.

56

There were pictures, obscure faces, on the white walls and there were tall windows with white curtains that riffled in a momentary breeze. One sweeping look was enough, he started to turn.

But Tricia stepped past him and without a word entered the room. She put the capsules back in the bottle and screwed the lid on. She picked up a book Wendell had not noticed lying on the floor and making a place on the table next to the bottles set it there. All this was a perfectly good housewifely thing to do, of course, but he noticed something. It was her face, the expression. It was not the scowl or any other one he remembered seeing. The expression was blankness itself, the very mask and stony gaze of boredom. In the seconds before her eyes focused on him again he knew he was wholly forgotten. He imagined a mind whose sole content was a bottle of pills and a book.

Expecting new inspiration he sat down to his novel that night. As it turned out this was a night like others in the past week when imagination failed him, when all he had written until now appeared to him in the light of flat banality and when, in the long intervals between his thoughts, he was conscious again of the stillness in the house. Sexual escapades, comic deceptions, buzzings in the neighborhood: there had to be more than these. He browsed another time through notes he had made of his conversations with Tricia. No use, not one thing that grabbed him. The more he thought the more appalling it all seemed. When every event and person and feeling was the common stock of any third-rate imagination, what in God's name was the use of his researches? Tricia, Mother, Joe, the whole lot of the denizens of this backwoods town. He lay in the dark with the pillow over his head.

Wendell did not give up, though. The next day he kept persuading himself that there might yet be something to unearth in Tricia, something so far withheld from him or maybe forgotten about, suppressed in the balmy depths of her unconscious. That evening, with a new line of questioning planned, he looked for her in the garden. She did not appear. She did not appear the next day either and he began to fear that by drawing her out too far he had left her feeling penitent.

He did see her from his window very late the following day. At the same time he got his solidest look so far at Joe, who came rolling in like any husband and left his car in front of the garage and leisurely mounted the gallery steps. He was a tall lean man who walked with a hump-shouldered slouch and wore a flowered sport-shirt that he might have acquired on one of those guided tours to the Caribbean. At the top of the steps Tricia was waiting for him, as was proper, with a kiss. But that kiss, with its suggestion of secret reparation for her transgression, seemed to Wendell in his present mood the seal of doom on his budding relationship with her.

It did not matter, and after supper he went at his novel again. One sentence and then another and he was against the blank wall already familiar to him. The end, he thought, laying his pencil down and turning to the window through which in first twilight he could see her garden with nobody in it. The stillness, like that sound as of drawn-out breath in a seashell, was gathering once more. He got up from his desk thinking about a holiday, that he would drive someplace. Remembering Atlanta he decided instead that he would settle for one of those *little* holidays.

He uncovered the box in the dirt floor of the chicken coop and found nothing but crumbs. He thought of Cat, that Cat worked at the car lot, and though it was nearly dark he set out walking fast. The car lot with its nightlights burning was deserted but Wendell by pure luck found him anyway. Stopped on the curb at Danford's Corner for a passing pickup truck he heard Cat speak to him. In the half-light against the brick wall behind him only Cat's shape was visible, but Wendell knew that shape—just as he knew the voice that had uttered nothing except his name. He took a step toward him, then another, and stopped.

"Looking for me?"

A little surprised Wendell said, "Yeah. I was." The streets, Wendell's glances showed him, were wholly empty now.

"Looking for your old job back?"

"Not that," Wendell said quietly. "I'm just wanting a little something. A dime bag . . . if you got it." Cat was twirling something, a small chain, on his finger, but for once he was looking steadily at Wendell.

"Ain't nothing I ain't got," Cat said. "You know that muse'm. Old barn down there behind it. You wait fifteen minutes and come down there. Come sly, though. Cross the railroad." He detached himself from the wall and went off springily down the street.

As if it was necessary, to make his waiting look innocent Wendell entered Baron's late-night grocery and bought a tube of toothpaste. As usual at night old Mr. Baron wanted to talk, and getting out of there without much delay always required some agility. Because he had known the old man to block the door he positioned himself, but even so Wendell was forced to give him an interval of apparent close attention. Mr. Baron's regular topic was the world's decline and particularly the decline of Turnbull, for most of which he blamed the university. Though he knew that Wendell was part of that enterprise he talked to him as if Wendell was one who sided with him. "If you had of knowed this town twenty year ago you'd see better. Them pointy-headed folks come in here and ruint it. It's some of them got so much hair till they looks like old bull buffaloes."

Mr. Baron had no upper teeth and all his s's and c's and f's were chirps and whistles that made the spit fly when he got excited. Everything was sliding downhill, he said, and he could not see any light at the end of the tunnel. Kids doping and fooling around like yard dogs in heat. And no respect, too *smart* for respect. Old ways and old folks shunted off to the boneyard like there never had been no such. All be gone pretty soon, all the old ones.

Here a small movement of his head interrupted the flow

but it led to a question. He knew Wendell lived next door to Miss Emma Harker and he wanted to know how the old lady was doing. "If you ain't met her, you ought to," he said. "There's one it'll sho hurt to lose. Fine a woman as is in the world. Generous woman . . . " He was warming to the subject but a blessed second customer intruded and set Wendell free.

Heading first up Mill Street toward his house he turned off and followed the alley in back of the stores along Danford. Some dogs barked at him in one of the back yards he crossed but he came out on the railroad without having seen anybody. Beyond, down ahead and invisible among cedar trees, was the museum. He held back. It was not only to let time, another minute or two, go by. For some reason he did not like the idea of Cat in the full darkness.

He pushed through bushes and in the park area, seeing the museum come bulking out of the night, he turned left. The sagging crest of the barn roof held its silhouette against the sky and he walked slow. Short of the barn a staggering gate stood open. In the dark beyond it Cat took shape a little bit at a time. Wendell was facing him.

"Dime bag ain't nothing."

"It's all I want."

"You got some friends, ain't you?"

"But they're gone off," Wendell said, thinking there was no real reason for his surprise at Cat's knowledge.

"They be back."

Something, a pigeon in the barn, made a gargling sound. In the starlight Wendell saw now that Cat had in his hand something too large for a dime bag. It looked like a box. When Cat held it out Wendell saw that it was half as big as a cigar box, wrapped around with twine.

"That's way more than I want."

"It's for a present. For old times, man."

Cat was still holding it out to him. Wendell set his tongue to say No, but the sound did not come. He took the box. It was too heavy. "I can't pay for all this."

"Ten dollar be fine."

"Ten?" Wendell said, trying to see his face. "It's got to be worth a hell of a lot more than that."

"No strings, man. Take it. We friends, ain't we? Bidness slow anyhow."

Wendell reached into his pocket and took out what was nearer to fifteen and gave it to him. "That's not near enough. I'm going to pay you what it's worth. Or bring most of it back to you."

"Don't matter."

One more little pause and Wendell turned and left.

He should have smelled something and in a way he did, but not with recognition. Taking a circular route and still not able to shake his troubled feeling, Wendell finally reached the house by a back way through the garden. It was as though he had already had knowledge of what would happen in that moment when he lifted his foot onto the stoop.

"Put your hands up, boy."

He did, with the box in his right one. That big pistol was glinting at him in the starlight and behind it, though shadowy, was a man the size of a boar hog standing upright. Wendell knew instantly who it was, had seen him a dozen times. It was half, the big half, of the Turnbull police force, Clarence (Dutch) Doolin, Chief. The other half was just then coming around the opposite corner of the house. But they were a long way from being a joke now.

"Let's have a look at what you got there."

Cautiously Wendell brought that hand down and extended it to Doolin. The small half of the force, with his pistol also trained on Wendell, was standing at Doolin's shoulder. "Look like a box," he said.

"Is a box," Doolin said. "Reckon what's in it?" He shook it and something rattled. "Hmnn. We better just step inside and get some light. You don't mind offering us a little hospertality, do you, boy?"

Wendell minded a great deal but he complied at once, keeping one hand up even while he opened the door and turned on the light over the table.

Without asking, Doolin sat down and put the box and his

pistol in front of him. Because of that other pistol trained on him Wendell had both his hands up again but he also had one eye on the box. Doolin was making a pause for the drama's sake, pursing and unpursing his fat lips. It was an effective pause, making Wendell even sicker than he had been.

"Hmnn. Wonder what's in here? What do you reckon it is, Gummy?"

"Rubbers," Gummy said. It was clear when he grinned why he was called Gummy.

"Naw. It's got a rattle."

"A snake," Gummy said.

"Not no snake. Well, we better look." His fat fingers undid the twine and opened the box. He dumped the contents onto the table and sat there looking at it all. Gummy gave a little whistle. For the first time in his life Wendell knew what sick really was.

"Well," Doolin finally said. He held a plastic bag dangling between his thumb and first finger. "Must be sugar for a birthday cake." Next it was a medicine bottle, from which Doolin shook three or four red capsules into the palm of his hand. "These here for bowel movements, I reckon," he said, drawing a chuckle from Gummy. And then the rest, three more bags and another bottle. Finally, "Hmnn," he said, putting the last bag down. "Look like about eight to ten worth, don't it, Gummy?"

"Sho do. If it ain't fifteen."

"Set down there, boy," Doolin said, looking at Wendell lugubriously from under his lids. "Take you a little last free rest."

This order came just about in time to keep Wendell from falling in a heap. Sitting down was a little help, though, and after a minute, in spite of the lidded eyes on him, introduced a wedge of something like clarity into his mind. It seemed he knew already that this was a plain setup but he could not get at the *why* of it. The reason for this lingering fuzziness appeared to be the ticking of that clock on top of the refrigerator which somehow inspired the words *last free rest* to keep speaking themselves in his memory.

"I feel sorry for you, boy. But you're got dead to rights and I got my duty."

Wendell did not see it in Doolin's eyes but suddenly he knew that something else was coming. It took a while. Gummy moved and settled into a posture of recline against the kitchen sink. Then it came, in tones of reluctant kindness. Doolin had not got halfway through before the shape of the whole sorry business dawned clear in Wendell's mind.

"He's the man owns the car lot," Wendell finally and faintly interrupted.

"That's him. Mr. Jason Farrow. Fine man. You can get him to guarantee you, I'll turn my face away." He paused and in a tone suddenly hardened said, "It's the onliest chance you got, boy."

So Wendell finally knew the name of the Big Man, the man that he, down in the ranks below Cat Bird, used to work for. Cat, the son of a bitch. And that big, that slick Farrow bastard behind his good-citizen badge rolling around up there in what was probably a fortune by now, dispatching his nasty little police force to shut the trap on Wendell. Why Wendell?

But the answer was close at hand. A veteran hustler and a university man rolled into one, just the kind of puppet needed for the ranks. Damned if he would fall in! Stuck here in this grubby county, risking his ass. There were bound to be weapons Wendell could use and in his anger he was already casting about for them when Doolin, watching him, said, "I 'spect he's home right now. I was you, I'd get over there quick as I could and go to begging. 'Cause when that jail door's shut, it's shut."

Watching Wendell he nodded his head, and then again, and then a third time. Wendell was still casting about for weapons but in his state of mind he could not fasten on a single one. Some instructions that he half-heard were coming at him. He saw the items on the table being gathered into the box and heard a few more words spoken in tones of gravity. Then he was sitting alone under the light bulb.

If Wendell had any real choice it did not come to him in the ten or so minutes while he kept sitting there at the table. Of course he could just run for it, which would be stupid. He could go on to jail and to court and scream with all his might about what had been laid on him and by whom—which might do them some damage but probably would not. His being a Corbin wouldn't help and neither would his checkered past if they got to work on that.

There was another thing. That same checkered past of his had given him some insight in the nature of this whole industry. It was not operated by gentlemen for humanitarian purposes and according to reliable report its unreliable membership were prone to fatal accidents. Like falling into wells, for instance. Envisioning this he did not relish the spectacle of himself afloat face-down at the bottom of a dark hole.

So much for his choices, then. So here he was, like a goat on a rope, hobbled—maybe even for the duration of a short life—in a place he barely would have chosen ahead of hell itself. With vengeance in his heart he cursed individually Doolin and Gummy and Cat Bird, not even saving one fresh obscenity for the real presiding bastard whose face he could not picture. At last, for release from rage still unexpressed, he came down even on Rathbone, who had brought him here. Slob, ass, pothead, with his murky brain full of Blake. He left the house with Rathbone positioned at least as high as Doolin on his list of avengees-to-be.

For all its distraction Wendell's brain had recorded the departing words of Doolin. These directed him to the alley that, in back of a row of mostly darkened houses, ran parallel to Rudd Street. There was no way to be mistaken about this house because Rudd dead-ended at its yard fence, a yard overgrown with big boxwoods and camellia bushes, and the house itself had a cupola on top. In fact from the alley, because of the bushes and trees in the yard, about all Wendell could see of the house was that cupola with its little spire against the pale night sky. A strange kind of place, he thought, as if it had been converted from a church building—and a little sinister. But this was surely his mood talking, a mood that by now had all but stifled his anger. In spite of what depended on the matter, he found himself wanting the absence of lights to mean that nobody was at home.

But there was a light, high up in the back of the house just under the cupola, illuminating part of the porch roof. Under the roof on the porch itself the darkness was such that he could see nothing whatever there, and the feeling that he was watched as he drew near had to have been his own imagining. To make sure, he stopped at the foot of the steps. He jumped. The voice, he realized afterwards, had said, "Come on up."

He did, wishing that at least he could see the shape of the man seated there in a blur against the wall. Stopped at the edge of the porch Wendell got hold of his voice. "I'm Wendell Corbin." This, though he now formed some other, defiant words in his head, was as much boldness as he could muster. His feeling, the particular character of it, was somehow familiar and suddenly he remembered that day when talking to Cat Bird at edge of the car lot he had felt himself being watched from the plate-glass window of the building. Now it made him think of the way a rabbit was said to fall helpless in front of a snake.

"Here's a chair. Set down."

Not a snake, though: a toad. This was Wendell's confused impression after he had sat down, after silent moments in which he was able to make out a little better certain features of the man seated a few steps away. He could see, or thought he could, that the man was thick and short in stature, rounded maybe, with a head planted squarely between rounded shoulders. If there was hair on the head he could not see it, any more than he could see whether it was true that the man had the kind of wide straight lipless mouth a toad had. Recalling the sound of the voice, Wendell now thought that even this reflected something of a toad's quality.

This was foolishness, the stress of the occasion. And in this silence and a darkness that made illusion easy and him unable to detect that the man seated there even so much as stirred in any part of his body, Wendell's disordered impressions were not too surprising. When Farrow spoke again, in a voice that did not at all resemble a toad's, Wendell felt like somebody suddenly given back to himself.

"What can I do for you, Wendell?"

So Farrow meant to play with him. What could he do but go along? "Chief Doolin said for me to come see you. About him catching me with some junk." He wished he had at least nerve enough to keep his voice natural. After a moment he also wished that Farrow would go ahead and answer, partly because the stillness seemed to threaten him with that toad vision again. To forestall it Wendell said, "He said you might help me."

"You're one of old Hap Corbin's kids, ain't you?"

Wendell was taken aback. "Yes."

"He dead yet?"

He paused again. "I'm not sure." For a second he wondered about it.

"I recollect him," Farrow's voice said. "Used to see him in Bison Springs sometimes, when I come in to town. We was the same kind." He fell into stillness again. "Only, I got out. Went everywhere, went high and low. Come back here and bought me this fine house. Fine one, ain't it?"

"Looks to be," Wendell mumbled.

"Own the car agency. Another one in Mobile. Member of the town council. And more besides. I do and go where and what I want to. Help and hurt who I want to."

Get to me, Wendell was thinking. But he waited out this silence too. It was long enough so that he became aware of cicadas sawing away and the fluttering cry of a screech owl somewhere.

"You live right there next door to old lady Harker."

It was not a question but Wendell murmured Yes. What else did Farrow know about him?

"You ever see her? Ever meet her?"

"Once."

"How'd that happen?"

"Her daughter-in-law invited me over. One afternoon."

The screech owl seemed to have moved closer to the house.

"A-ris-to-crat," Farrow said, curiously, pronouncing each syllable though not with any passion. "Still hanging on." In a voice that seemed to drift away he added, "Just to make me trouble."

Wendell waited. Farrow did not return to the subject and Wendell was left to wonder about it later.

"I need a boy like you. Smart, educated boy. One got experience along with it."

Of course he would know all this—from Cat, the son of a bitch, if in no other way. What disturbed Wendell more was a sort of hunch or intuition that would not explain itself. It was as though Farrow had hold of him by some other means than the crude trap in which he had caught him. It came to Wendell's mind that he had not ceased to feel this way since the moment he set foot on the porch and thought about a helpless rabbit and a snake. That he had better be on guard even about his secret thoughts was another notion that came to him.

"Ever think about getting rich?"

"No," Wendell murmured. He had thought about it but never as a possibility.

"That's about all there is, getting rich," Farrow said. "Except maybe getting even." For the first time Wendell saw him move and, he believed, look directly at him. Farrow said, "You're where rich is at, now. It ain't penny ante no more. Just do everything I tell you and keep your mouth shut. Tight shut."

After a moment Wendell realized that this was it, his dismissal. No question, no call for his assent, and he was on his feet as if Farrow had secretly pulled one of his strings. He was down the steps and a few paces on his way before he experienced what had quite abandoned him over the last half hour, his defiant anger. But he was well out of the alley and halfway home before he began again to rage inside himself.

In his bed in the dark, Wendell could not sleep for rehearsing the whole sorry chain of events and in his wilder moments imagining his fists smashing faces. But Farrow was where his mind stuck. Having never really seen him, Wendell kept envisioning a toad's face, and there was an unsatisfactory ambiguity about the effect on it of his imagined blows. Anyway this was childish. Also childish, disgusting now to recall, was the image of his quaking self made speechless in that man's presence. Why? He writhed in his bed. No, his vengeance would come about in some way more punishing than any blows. In the meantime, though, Farrow had him, did he not?

Wendell finally went to sleep, though he kept waking up and to his surprise remembering what Farrow had said about getting rich. Money. Would lots of money be so bad? Before daylight came he was sleeping better.

VIII

Wendell spent the next couple of days in nervous antici-
pation, expecting word of some kind, by some means. But
his rage, though now and again screwing itself back to its
original pitch, was generally moderated and much of the
time absent altogether. These were the intervals when he
thought about money and having lots of it. He could leave
this place, this state, this country if he had to, thumbing his
nose from a jet airplane somewhere. Another thought that
encouraged complacency was that now he would at least
have something to busy his hands. His self was lousy company. At times he hated it and entertained even the notion
that the insupportable presence of Rathbone and Alice would
be better than nothing at all in the house.

About dark in the evening of the second day he sat down
with his novel, at the kitchen table for a change. It was as
before: nothing, not even one sentence would come. He
watched the clock on the refrigerator and wondered if somewhere in the house, in a littered drawer maybe, there might
be something for his imagination, or at least for a little holiday. He was just at the point of getting up when he heard a
sound, and stiffened. It was on the stoop outside, a footfall.

Except by glimpses from his window he had not seen
Tricia for most of a week and in fact had thought about her
only fitfully. But here she suddenly was, his Muse, standing
at the back door in the dusk. If now his excitement was not
entirely literary he passed it off as that. He just remembered
to put his novel on the shelf behind him before he turned to
the door.

Wendell was as much surprised at her condition as at her presence. Her eyes were wet, there were little tear streaks at the corners, and when she tried to speak, nothing at all came out. Opening the screen he said, "What's the matter?" This inspired another vocal effort but the sound she produced was not a word.

"Is somebody dead?" He would see that it was not anything like that. "Come on in," he said and reached and took her by the elbow, drawing her into the kitchen. She was wearing shorts, very short.

"I wish she was." At least the sounds were words now. She stood in the light with her wet eyes looking around her as if bewildered at the strange place she had happened into.

"Mother, you mean?"

"I hate her."

"Tell me about it. Here, sit down." He handed her to a chair opposite his own at the table. "I'll get you some coffee."

"All right."

The coffee on the stove was still hot and he quickly poured a cup for her and refilled his own, hearing her, behind him, make a noise in her throat. He set the cups down and for privacy shut the door and drew the curtain over the pane. He was excited. It was because here maybe was a scene coming up, a big one. From his chair he said, "Okay. Tell me about it."

"She's . . ." Evidently it was inexpressible.

"What happened? Drink some coffee, it'll calm you down." She wiped both eyes with her fingertips. A lock of hair that looked almost yellow blond in this light had fallen cunningly onto her brow. She took a sip from her cup and seemed to feel better. "It was just . . . I don't know how to tell it."

"Try."

Her lips shut tight, and opened. "It started about me wearing shorts. She used words . . ."

He waited. "What kind of words? Not cuss words?"

"Like *vulgar*. That's what *I* am, vulgar. Everything I do.

Or don't do. She's got a kind of sneaky way of mocking, so you can't come back at her."

Wendell wanted details. "What did she mock you about?"

"Reading Nietzsche . . . for one thing. She calls him Nitch, she thinks that's clever. Reading him is a sign of my *values.* That's what she meant. I ought to be reading the Bible. Or *something* proper. Something a *lady* would read."

"That what she told you tonight?"

"Yes. In her way. And more besides."

"This one must have been a humdinger. What else?"

"That I'm not a good mother." Tricia's blue eyes flashed.

"Just out like that?"

"That Little Joe ought to be home, learning family things. Her things, she means. She wants to tell him about 'the old plantation.' She's always telling him about that, like it wasn't all a hundred years ago. She thinks she raised him. She didn't, though, *I* did. And he's a plain nice boy and not any snobby *aristocrat.*"

The word, with the strong hiss she put in the middle of it, touched something in his mind. That was Farrow's word too for the old woman. "That's the right spirit," Wendell said, thinking about Farrow.

"She's ugly about everbody. Everybody that's *alive.* She thinks nobody but her is any good anymore." Tricia took a determined swallow of coffee. Her eyes had dried but there was still a brightness in them. "Sometimes she's even ugly about her own son, that's so devoted to her. Because he's a salesman."

Wendell remembered something else. He hesitated. "I heard her being ugly about Jason Farrow."

"Oh she's uglier about him than anybody."

"How so?"

"She says he's scum. She says terrible things about him. And after he helped Joe get the job he's got now."

Wendell paused for a moment and said, "What *things* about him?"

"That he's a drug dealer. Things like that. That she makes up out of pure meanness."

He just stared at Tricia, vaguely conscious of the blue eyes, a heightened blue, looking back at him. He finally said, "Where'd she get that idea?"

"No place. She reads all the horrible stories in newspapers and magazines. And makes up more. Oh, and she had a dream about him. A dream!" The eyes flashed a little brighter. "She loves horrible things. Like about the Farnsworth boy that she won't stop talking about. And just yesterday there was something about a businessman in Birmingham. That got her started on Mr. Farrow all over again."

"I see." He looked into his cup and, lifting it, took his first sip of the tepid coffee, thinking. He could tell Farrow. He could. He said, "What does Joe think about all that?"

"Joe doesn't *think* anything. Besides, he's always gone." Her mouth turned down at the corners, tensing her lips. "The first thing he does when he gets home is go up to her room like a little boy. He'd put up with anything from *Mama*. One of these days . . ."

He waited to hear *what*, but Tricia only lifted the cup to her mouth. The tress of hair flowing over one eyebrow now had his attention. "One of these days, what?" When after waiting again he got no answer, he said, "It seems to me you put up with an awful lot from her, yourself."

Her eyes flashed again. "I didn't tonight."

He still liked the way that lock hung there, about to veil one eye. It had all but captured his attention from the matter that just moments ago he was thinking so heavily about. Rather mechanically, because his interest here too had suddenly flagged, he said, "Did you do something special tonight?"

"I walked out on her," she said proudly.

"First time, huh? That's progress."

"And I told her from now on she could give herself her old shot. She could, too. Her hands are not all that stiff like she pretends."

72

Remembering, Wendell asked, "Did you shoot her in the same place tonight?"

"I don't know."

"You said you did sometimes. You know, maybe she's right and you do do it on purpose. It could be subconscious."

Tricia obviously considered this something to think about and he saw a new expression gathering in her eyes.

"I'm always glad afterwards. So maybe I do do it on purpose." Suddenly that expression, all over her face, put Wendell wonderfully in mind of a new-fledged desperado. He was amused but he was more than only amused. His eyes went back to the lock of hair, then down to those full lips. He said,

"A sign you're breaking out. Of your old self, I mean. You have to be bold. Liberate yourself . . . like Nietzsche says."

It was just about here, Wendell later thought, that his itch translated itself into an intention as clear as that of any old rake. It had the impulse of perfectly natural lust, all right, but other, less honest causes also made a contribution. His present tension played a part and so did his general frustration and boredom. But the least creditable cause had to be an obscure but compelling urge to tear the scales from her eyes, to expose past all concealment the Tricia there behind the phony mask. Maybe even Mother was in it, and a kind of revenge therefore an ingredient in the brew. He would come to think of it finally as in fact a devil's brew, but for now he was intent on the business at hand.

It was not as difficult as he expected. With an absentee husband she did not care about much and the old dragon Mother to defy and nothing serious in the way of principles, her built-in defenses were less than formidable. It was mainly a matter of stimulating the right glands and the means to this did not evade Wendell's cunning. The route in was through her *intellect*. So he let Zarathustra lead him, to the accompaniment of some intellectual music, some Wagner, that he put on the stereo. They were in the living room by then, on the sofa where he had enticed her with promise of yet deeper instruction in the mysteries of the Seer. He had switched on only the one lamp at the end of the sofa, a light so dim he could barely see the page, and leaning closer than necessary to the pink shell-like ear he read in his huskiest voice the seductive words. Like:

> The hour when you say, "What matters my virtue?" As yet it has not made me rage. How weary am I of my good and evil! All that is poverty and filth and wretched contentment!

And:

> More honestly and purely speaks the healthy body that is perfect and perpendicular: and it speaks of the meaning of the earth. Thus spoke Zarathustra.

And this while the music, to cadences as slow and majestic as the Ubermensch's stride, bore the mighty Siegfried to his tomb. But it was in the middle of the "Liebestod" that Wendell made his move.

The issue held a surprise. He had anticipated a formal if not a vigorous resistance and as he read along, with reverent pauses for bits of explanation, he kept considering what his strategy ought to be. The naked thigh nearest to him, fleshy and wonderfully colored like tinted cream, would be, he decided, his starting place. When finally with sly hesitation he laid his hand on it he was expecting the hand to be rejected once or twice for sure. Instead Tricia acted as if she did not know it was there. She said, gazing into the near-darkness across the room, "That music's so nice. It just seems to go along with Nietzsche, doesn't it?"

"Does, doesn't it?" Wendell said from a strangled throat. He moved his hand, just a little. That did it. She was on his neck.

He did not know afterwards whether she had enjoyed it as much as he had. Plain defiance, he was sure, played a hefty part in her fall, but whether this had inflamed or diminished her zest in the act would have to be answered by her. When the going got good, Wendell, working away with Ubermenschian energy, was mostly pretty dim about things not actually happening inside the periphery of his own flesh. He did know, however, that the pleasure was all the greater for the fragments of pure consciousness that kept flashing through his head. This was little Tricia, he thought, groaning on the sofa. And, thrusting, he thought: *This* for your Zarathustra. Once, aware of a cry, he imagined with a surge of lust Mother listening from a window over there. That, Wendell believed, had in fact been his critical moment.

He was thoroughly wilted afterwards and he lay in a heap against the end of the sofa watching her put her clothes back on. She did it without speaking. Her face was turned away from him and he envisioned a cloud over it and maybe tears of shame and conscience at the thought of her fall. Alas for virtue lost. But he was surprised. All dressed again, she showed him a face that was not only unclouded but positively complacent. She looked at Wendell as if his nakedness was nothing out of the ordinary. He reckoned that conscience would smite her later on but he was still surprised. He said, "You're not sorry, I hope."

She did not say anything but she shook her head No.

"Don't be. I'd like to see you think of it as a milestone."

Her mouth made an ambiguous movement. To his surprise she got up from the sofa and headed out through the kitchen. Thinking what a nice or at least sexy shape she had, he called after her, "I hope you don't mean not to come back." But she passed out of sight through the door without any acknowledgment.

Too sleepy to move, Wendell lay there naked on the sofa and speculated about the effect on her and whether it might spell trouble for him. He thought of the old woman in the kitchen and with satisfaction about how this little romp with her daughter-in-law was, though hidden from her, a good hard slap across her arrogant mouth. Then he thought about

Joe, with horns, driving places. But he was too drowsy for thought and he let his body sink on down into sleep.

"Man, you look like a plucked chicken. Glad I ain't white all over like that."

Wendell heard this on his way up from the depths and when he started fully awake he saw a man standing over him, black. It was Cat.

"You go nekid 'round here all the time?" the bird voice asked him.

Wendell was still another moment getting a good breath in him. When he did, lifting himself upright he said, "You dirty son of a bitch." He had not paused to consider his words and in the wake of them he watched Cat's face with some anxiety. He remembered his old impression of a side to Cat that was a good deal darker than his face. But Cat did not show it to him. Wendell saw only the accustomed flickering changing face, good humored.

"Sorry 'bout that. Wasn't none of my idea."

"You did it, though. Set that trap for me." Wendell wished he had his clothes on.

"My hands done it, maybe. But it was the will of him which set me to it. It was the Big Controller hisself. When the big voice speak . . ."

"Don't start that stuff."

" . . . us little folks jumps. Which is what you better do. He said for you to come over there."

"Now?"

"That's it. Ain't me saying it. I just come bearing the word. So now I done it." He turned quickly and on his way out through the kitchen called back, "You better put some clothes on. He won't like nekid."

Wendell put his clothes on but he did so thinking that it was only because being dressed around the house was the accustomed thing. He thought he would not bother to go tonight or, if he did, he would not be in a hurry about it. He even sat down at the kitchen table and, reaching for his novel behind him, started thinking about Tricia and what he would write now. The back door was standing open. He got up and went out onto the stoop. After a minute he descended the steps and kept on walking.

Up to a point it was like a rerun of the scene two nights before. As then, he came from the alley and approached the house from behind. That one same light high up under the cupola was burning and the darkness on the back porch made it impossible for him to see anything up there. Once more when he stopped at the foot of the steps the voice told him to come on up. He even had that helpless feeling again and the eerie impression that something like a big toad with clothes on was seated a few steps away from him. What Wendell needed, he thought, was to see Farrow in daylight, or some light, and so clear his head of this distorting foolishness. Meanwhile, even hearing that screech owl once again, he sat like a stone waiting out Farrow's silence.

"Want you to do me a favor." He surprised Wendell with a perfectly human voice.

"You know where Appleton's at? County seat of Upjohn, little place. It's a old airstrip four miles from there which I got a use for." It was, Farrow said, on a cotton plantation that was out of business now but the sheriff up there kept his eye on it because a few years ago the Feds had almost caught somebody trying to use it. Wendell had heard about this kind of thing. They got the stuff in South America and flew it in at night, whole big planeloads of it. So this was not any penny-ante operation he was getting dragged into. Besides, thinking about the Feds in it made him more nervous than he already was. Damn it, he wouldn't do it. But he did not say anything, even though Farrow's voice had now stopped. Wendell had heard a thousand screech owls in his life but never one with a voice as shuddery as this one close by somewhere.

"Your business is seeing to that sheriff. Your first business, anyhow."

What? Wendell thought, like a scream in his head. Did

Farrow mean, *kill* him? He barely managed to say, "How?"

"Money. It's a thousand in that sack on the floor there by you. Give him that. Then it's four more thousand coming to him when it's all wound up. Tell him that."

This was relief, all right, but not enough, even with that much money in it. "What if he won't? He'll put me in jail. He *could* be honest."

"Nah. Like five hundred might make him hold off awhile. Not this much. He ain't held five thousand dollars in the best dream he ever had. He'll have them praying at church for you."

Maybe, maybe not. The hell he would.

"Grissom's his name. You go up there tomorrow. Then come see me again. I'll have something else for you."

By tomorrow Wendell would be on the road, by God, too long gone to catch. This was what he was thinking in the secrecy of his own head and yet Farrow's next words, making Wendell blink, might just as well have been a direct answer.

"Don't go letting your mind run, Wendell," he said, and paused—a heavy pause. "Get your mind right. Best way to do that is, not think about nothing but the money coming to you. Good money. Five thousand ought to be about it. When the thing's all done, I mean."

Wendell blinked again, trying in the aftershock of Farrow's little mind-reading trick to get a hold on this last thing said to him. "Five thousand?" He barely heard his own voice.

"When it's all done. This-here is the one and only money tree, boy. Just hold on tight." Then silence once again. "Don't forget that sack there."

This was Wendell's dismissal and taking the sack he stood up. But Farrow had one more thing to say. "I can give you a car if you don't like taking that p'fessor's."

He knew that too. It took Wendell a moment, before he turned and descended the steps, to answer, "His'll do fine."

Farrow had to have been spying on him all along—through Cat, no doubt. But this was only part of the explanation and not the part that most disturbed Wendell, for Cat had no way to spy inside his head. Though neither did anybody else, Wendell told himself without ridding himself of the eerie feeling about Farrow. It was just a feeling, foolishness, with nothing better for evidence than the man's shrewd guess at what was in Wendell's thoughts. All he needed was a good daylight look at Farrow.

This last, however, as Wendell discovered before he went to sleep that night, was not the only remedy for his distress. There were his worries, at one point his near-panic, about the sheriff tomorrow. But finally he got his mind's eye fastened on a remedy that was even more effective and that he took to sleep with him. Five thousand dollars! It was a fortune, impossible. But the money in the sack, that he had counted, was like an earnest. He would be rich even if it was impossible. A rich Corbin, rich.

IX

For the simple reason that no known Corbin had ever in the least expected or even seriously hoped for such a thing Wendell had never thought about getting rich. In his family tradition money was something one got in limited amounts and then spent and went a little hungry until some more came along. But in this case it was a real and solid expectation, made a virtual certainty in his mind when, the following night on Farrow's dark back porch, he was handed an envelope that turned out to contain twenty genuine fifty-dollar bills, all for him to keep. He felt himself a changed man. Certainly this new feeling about himself played no small part in feeding the energy that carried him through the next weeks.

His new career had had a shaky start, however. At least *shaky* was the right word for Wendell's condition as he drove into the town of Appleton that day and circled the square and found a parking space in front of a drugstore across the street from the courthouse. The town was somewhat bigger than Turnbull and Bison Springs but it was still territory made familiar by its square of low old-brick storefronts facing a squat dingy courthouse with pecan trees on the lawn where elderly bumpkins lounged in the shade. This was some comfort, especially when, getting out of an aging Chevrolet like others in sight, he reflected that there was nothing about him to draw notice. Once a redneck, always a redneck, at least in appearance. Naturally he still knew how to talk it, and also walk it, and he experienced the alarming ease with which he could drop back into the old character. For the first time he realized that his origin had been one of the things that caught Farrow's eye.

With the wad of money ingeniously situated beneath his shirt under his armpit Wendell stepped onto the courthouse lawn like any innocent rube. Inwardly, though, the closer he came to that ground-level door in the courthouse wall marked Sheriff's Office, the more he began to shake. A small event en route did not help matters.

In circling the square Wendell had seen the cluster of men, maybe a dozen of them, standing not too distant from that door in the courthouse wall but he had not taken note of the fact that they were in the clutches of a preacher. His mistake now, with the thought to make himself look natural, was stopping for a couple of minutes to seem to listen in on the harangue. It was the usual stuff, alternating threats and promises, hellfire with the devil or heavenly bliss with Jesus, delivered by a preacher different from most only in that he was undersized and too young to be taking the old claptrap seriously. But he had a big voice and, for Wendell, this seemed to be the trouble. Instead of being insulated by his hatred of such preachers, or any preachers, he found himself listening, really listening. For some moments there, while the little creature shouted and furiously gesticulated, Wendell experienced what felt like conscience in him, or the terror of hellfire, raising tremors somewhere in the region of his heart.

These tremors lasted only a minute or two, for suddenly, like a minor stroke of salvation, a car horn sounded and revealed to Wendell what the source of his trouble really was. Open windows flanked that door in the wall, assuring no refuge within from the trumpeting voice. He could see himself. There he would be, proposing a bribe in an office resonant with Jesus and the devil. Damn this preacher's mouth! By the time he got through, which must have been close to half an hour, Wendell was not sure but what the man really had got to him with his hellfire.

When he got admitted to the little office inside, it was his first thought that the sheriff, seated at his desk with his back to the open window, had not yet recovered from having his soul touched by the recent eloquence. Wendell had set himself to meet a pair of flinty eyes in the kind of face small-town sheriffs were supposed to have. Instead this face though beefy wore a benevolent fatherly expression and regarded Wendell with eyes that looked as if they might have just now dried up after a good cry. He seemed for all the world like a church member greeting with brotherly love at the end of a service. For Wendell's purpose this, he thought, was a good deal worse than what he had anticipated. His heart did sink when he noticed on the walls not only no guns but, on one wall, a calendar picture of a haloed Jesus looking up to heaven.

"What can I do for you, son," the sheriff said mildly, and Wendell saw his hand let go of what he desperately hoped was not a Sunday school bulletin. When Wendell could not answer, the sheriff said, "Just have a seat there, rest your bones."

"It's . . . private," Wendell managed to say.

"Sholy. Push that old door shut."

He sat down as invited but he found that his tongue was like a stone in his mouth. He would not do it, he would think up something else to say. The sheriff leaned back in his swivel chair and, looking benevolent, folded his hands over his belly. His khaki shirt was stretched tight there, like Santa Claus's coat.

"You got the look of a young man on a mission," the sheriff said after a moment. "I seen you out the window while ago. Just listening. Listening to the Word. Noticed you special 'cause I couldn't place you. I said to myself, 'There's a young fellow on serious business. Might be the Lord's business.' That what it is?"

Wendell mutely shook his head and then, in confusion, started to say Yes. But what would follow the Yes? Then he was surprised to see something different in the sheriff's expression, something shrewd. It started a cold feeling crawling up his backbone.

"Look like you brought something along with you. Under your arm there."

"Where?" Wendell said.

The shrewd look was gone, changed back to benevolence. "Look like a bump there. What is that? Something for me?"

Wendell's mouth worked but nothing came out. He felt like a man teetering on the edge of a high place.

"Wouldn't be money, would it? For me?"

"It's a thousand dollars," Wendell blurted, feeling himself leave the edge. "From a man. And four more thousand to come."

A long stillness, in which he was vaguely aware of a typewriter clicking beyond the shut door, finally ended in a decisive blink of the sheriff's eyes.

"Five thousand?"

Wendell nodded stiffly.

"What's that man want for it?"

"That airstrip." Wendell was watching the sheriff's face so tensely that he forgot to continue.

"Uh huh," the sheriff finally said. "Want to bring in a little cargo, huh?"

Wendell just looked at him, falling, waiting on his fate.

"You're in trouble, boy."

It was the end of a long fall and Wendell had landed stunned in this chair. Through a haze he saw the sheriff stroking his chin, beginning to work his mouth.

"But you look like the *makings* of a good boy," he slowly said. "I'm inclined to overlook it. Let's say, six. That ought to be just about enough to finish our new church with."

This interlude with Sheriff Grissom was a confidence builder for Wendell. He had some shaky moments later, though never any in which his resourcefulness seriously deserted him. At bottom, he believed, his new maturity came from an expanded conciousness of the real value of what he was to get out of all this: money. In the past he had naïvely thought of money as only something with which to buy things for one's self, which seemed good enough. Now he saw that it would not only buy *things*, it would buy anything, including people, including even natural enemies, and was therefore as good for offense as it was for defense. This was why nothing succeeded like success and it was why rich people strutted through the world. The odds seemed pretty good now that he could become one of them. So, on the day following his real initiation into crime, on the kind of laconic instructions from Farrow that he was already getting used to, he made the hour-long drive to Montgomery in a state of excitement.

It was room 16 at the Old Dixie Inn on the east side of the city and clearly he was expected. In fact he was greeted at the door, by a middle-aged man who he already knew was named Halloway and called Hal, as if he had been a family member. Hal's first words were "Great to see you, Wendell boy," and he followed this with a deeply felt inquiry about Wendell's health, as if Wendell had been one of the frailer family members. Hal was amazed to learn that he was a graduate student in English and even paused momentarily to fasten on Wendell a look of shining admiration. In real life, as he put it, he was, himself, into moving and storage but he had always admired English, it being his native language. Wendell did not know what was characteristic of people who were into moving and storage but he wondered whether it could be that many of them wore cream-and-blue-checked sport jackets like Hal's and luminous yellow ties with tiepins that said HOPE on them. He was able to see why Hal admired English, given the rate at which he used it. Wendell did not perceive until later, when he became aware of the cunning behind the appearance, that all this was part of a role portraying the brainless aspiring redneck. It was meant to be a professional disguise but Hal apparently liked it so much that he was always forgetting it was not real.

There were, as Wendell had been noticing, two other members of the family connection also in the room. At last, with a sudden expression of pain at his own discourtesy, Hal turned and with apologies introduced them to Wendell. They did not seem much wounded by the delay. The one nearest, longer than the bed he lay on, removed from under his head a hand about the size of a shovel blade and with a mumbled "Ho" lifted it in greeting. His size, along with the muscles his T-shirt did not hide, suggested—rightly, as it turned out—that he was or had been an athlete. In fact he was an ex-linebacker on the university football team but the something familiar about him was only because Wendell had unhappily met the likes of him in a couple of his freshman English classes. Calvin Walls was his name. It really was his name. Of all the people Wendell was to meet in the organization this was the only one whose name he ever knew for certain to be authentic.

Evan McCauley, the man propped on the farther bed with the magazine on his knees, acknowledged the introduction only by turning, for a moment, world-weary eyes on Wendell. He wore a loose pale gray rayon shirt with the sleeves rolled back halfway to his elbows and he had a small black mustache that might have been in imitation of Hitler's. His appearance also pointed to what he was, or was said to be: a rich young man, a Kentuckian, in flight from the boredom of his father's millions. He was also a snot who Wendell instantly disliked.

This, Wendell's first introduction to personnel of The Company—as it was always referred to—left him confused about the type of people he was now involved with. In the next couple of weeks he discovered that this was a perfectly representative sampling, that The Company was composed of no *type* at all. There were rich and poor, crooked and respectable, black and white, vicious and kind. In fact the personnel amounted to a true cross-section of the Genus Americanus. To a man of conscience this was bound to be a comforting realization: what one did along with everybody else was just another manifestation of the American Way, even if a more than commonly risky one. But to a man as economics-minded as Wendell was in process of becoming, this fact also had a distressing side. An industry like this one necessarily depended on being exclusive, and with every kind of person and more and more of them getting into it every day, where finally were the customers to come from?

Wendell first thought about this while listening to Hal on the drive to the airstrip that evening. They went in Hal's Lincoln Continental, two-toned yellow and white and about four years old, a car chosen, Wendell later guessed, to further dramatize Hal's rising-redneck image. It had a back seat big enough to accommodate both McCauley, looking bored and far-away in his corner, and Walls, who was asleep all over the remaining four or five feet of space. Throughout the drive neither one of them said a word but this might have been because Hal never once stopped talking.

Hal was as proud of The Company as if he were its president, and Wendell learned on that trip most of what he was ever going to know about it in general. He did not learn who the president was or any facts about those at the top but he doubted that Hal had any such knowledge either. He kept thinking about Farrow in this connection. Could it be possible that he, that eerie bastard squatted like a toad in the dark of his back porch, was the Big Man of them all?

"Now you see," Hal said, his eyes cutting back and forth from Wendell to the road ahead of them, "the way we're set up, it's three main levels. There's the boys that bring it in. All by airplane now, big ones. Some of them DC-6's. Carry fifteen, twenty thousand pounds of stuff. Bring it up from Colombia. That's way down there in South America. That's level number one."

Level number two was the boys responsible for locating and fixing up the airstrips, and also refueling the airplanes after delivery. "That's my job," Hal said. "A big one, too. Now you'd think, being into moving and storage, I'd be on the third level, which is hauling the stuff off to the wholesalers. And I used to be. But that was too much of a pointer. Orders come down from the top and now I'm a airstrip man.

That's what you're into right now, under me. And Walls and McCauley too," he said, pointing with a thumb toward the silent pair in back. "And a lot more people besides."

Everything was big—airplanes, trucks, personnel, money, especially the money. The smallest figure Hal mentioned was $50,000, which was the amount The Company had paid to bribe the Drug Enforcement Administration employee in Washington who had furnished the list of DEA radio frequencies that Hal had in the address book he took out of an inside pocket to show Wendell. For this little book, Hal said, in twenty-four hours he could get $10 million from any one of ten rival companies. And there was the company kitty where they kept $2 or $3 million just in case a couple of airplanes or trucks or something had to be abandoned. A couple of good loads and, shucks, a few million wasn't to fret about. Talk about the oil business. Rich? "Boy," he said, "you're in the place where 'rich' is at."

As Hal went on about the millions, even his language grew inflated. "We make sure our money flow takes on a downhill posture," he said, explaining how the money for the payoffs flowed, in a never-ending process, from the final distributor back down through all the levels to the starting place in Columbia, where the same round got under way again. By now, taking it all in, Wendell's mind had grown a little dazzled. Even the flat country they were driving through, with its pine woods and green pastures and cotton fields, began to have for him a tint of gold in its coloration.

But suddenly there was a small break, or merely a bump maybe, in the current of things. It came of the slight but very noticeable change in Hal's tone and lasted just long enough for him to say, "'Course we look for all our people to be loyal. Yes sir, loyal." Then he was back in the old stream, telling Wendell about the lawyers The Company had who would take care of anybody who got in trouble. But Wendell had taken his meaning and for some minutes this meaning caused him to view the passing landscape in a rather more sober light. This was his first moment of unambiguous consciousness that Hal was a man who went about in disguise.

They drove through the middle of Appleton, slowly, passing the courthouse, where Wendell saw the same bumpkins lounging but no hellfire preacher haranguing a crowd. After that there were about three miles of farms and scattered farmhouses and then a stretch where woods alternated with fields mostly overgrown with pine saplings. Just before sunset Walls got out to open a sagging gate. They drove up a slight incline through old water oak and cedar and pecan trees and saw after a minute the plantation house with its tall columns. From a distance the house looked intact but up closer Wendell could see that it was a burnt-out shell. He did not know what caused the pang of melancholy that made him wonder about the family, what had happened to them: they were nothing to him and his kind. But he did feel it and he did wonder as they turned onto a dirt track and passed the house and he heard Hal say, "Gone with the wind."

They passed a couple of barns and a roofless cabin and bumped for half a mile through a sedge field. Wendell could see the metal hangar before they got there but not the airstrip until they approached the edge of it. The strip was some hundreds of yards long, made of asphalt, ending each way against a screen of pinewoods. Hal drove the length of it, pointing out each pit and crack where vegetation grew. "Got to cut out the bushes and fill them. Plain old clay'll do."

They walked around the airstrip for a while listening to Hal give instructions about reflectors and Q-beam spotlights and air-ground radios and countersurveillance points. He must have named a dozen people unknown to Wendell, all of whom had to be here on the big night—and previous nights too, to get ready. About a week, he said; it depended. "But you boys get down here tomorrow night for sure and get started. You get them here, McCauley. And a couple more if you need them."

McCauley, despite his appearance of bored inattention,

nodded. It was the nearest thing to an energetic movement Wendell had seen him make.

That was a long and exhausting week. Wendell spent the first three nights at the airstrip with McCauley, Walls, and a small swarthy man called Venutti, who said he was from Detroit and used be a shoe salesman. It was more work then Wendell had expected. There were a great many of those holes in the asphalt surface and some of them were big enough to require a whole load of clay from the pickup truck they used. They kept the truck lights off. They used only flashlights and they even talked quietly, when they talked. After each load three of them would go back with the truck to the clay bank and the fourth one would stay behind to finish the smoothing and packing down. This was Wendell's job.

Sometimes he got finished well before the truck came back and stood propped on his shovel looking and listening toward where they had vanished in the sedge field, but he could hardly ever see or hear them until they started back. It was quiet then, quieter than a night ought to be and darker until the moon came up. Very late the third night he watched the moon, a reddish half of a moon, go down over the burnt-out house half a mile away. Suddenly he had that feeling of melancholy again. What had happened to the family? He had a groundless notion that something bad had happened to them and that, for some reason, it had to do with him. Or was it something that was going to happen? When they left there just before daylight Wendell was feeling nervous, and when, an hour later, he lay in bed in his room he seemed unable to make his eyes stay shut.

The next night, after waiting until almost nine for instructions, he was summoned by telephone to another meeting at a different motel in Montgomery. Of the twelve faces in the room, including several that were either foreign-looking or black, Wendell knew three. Venutti, he noticed, was not there but a little later he heard mention of him. Meanwhile they all sat or stood around the room listening to Hal, who had on either the same clothes as before or else identical ones. The only thing different about him was that now he was smoking a cigar, adding to the already nearly unbreathable atmosphere.

"It's on for Thursday night," Hal said. "Plane's took off for Colombia, South America. Be there two days. Things looking good so far. One little hitch, been straightened out." This was when Wendell noticed on a dresser at the back of the room what he recognized as a scanner, with a small red light that jumped around on the screen from one frequency to another.

Calling names, Hal handed out written instructions. "Learn them and burn them," he said. "Be shore and burn them."

Wendell was glad for the ones he got. He was still feeling nervous and his instructions for tomorrow were that he go to Atlanta and buy, for some reason, two industrial-type vacuum cleaners. This affected him like a small vacation promised, a whole day away from it all. Then he was fingering another idea. Atlanta was a hundred miles away, a long headstart. What if he ran? But his thoughts were interrupted.

Seated on the floor with his back against the wall was a man with thin red hair and a bulbous disfigured nose. The word of his that had struck Wendell was the word *narc*, and now he noticed that everybody in earshot had hushed and was looking intently at the man. "It's what I heard," the man said in a Yankee accent. "Somebody new, I think." Wendell felt eyes turned on him. The man said, "I heard Flanagan named. Venutti too. Neither one of them's here tonight."

There was silence. Venutti stood focused in Wendell's mind—small, obliging, with slick swarthy face. In these moments his nervousness screwed itself up a notch or two and when, just as people were starting to leave, an envelope was handed to him he did not even think to open it.

He did think to open it finally, in his car, and it was a thousand dollars. Another thousand! Before long this second windfall had all but overridden his nervousness and by the time he got home that night thoughts about Venutti and narcs were coming at him only in fits and starts. After all he was in with people who knew what they were doing. Soon he had stopped even playing with the notion of making a run for it.

He went to Atlanta. On the night of the day after that he was back at the airstrip putting up stakes that, the next night, would have reflectors on them. In the hangar now were two big van-type trucks with fuel tanks in the back and items like pumps and radio antennas and his two vacuum cleaners. What looked like the whole crowd showed up at one time or another and talked or fooled with equipment in a sort of weird hushed way. Maybe not the whole crowd, though, for he never saw Venutti. Wendell did not let himself think about this. He got all his stakes set, with hooks on them, and helped change a tire on one of the trucks. About daylight he reached home exhausted and slept into the afternoon. Then there was nothing to do but wait around for night, the big night.

It was slow waiting. He paced and turned the TV on and off again and looked out the windows. Once he saw Tricia on the way from her car to the back gallery. She had stayed out of his mind wonderfully through the past week but now his thoughts converged on her. She had what seemed to be groceries in her arms, the look of a wife about her domestic business. Was she "ruing the day"? Just then he would have bet she was, with secret wifely tears for her fall and little talks with God in which she vowed purity white as snow henceforth and forever. A spiritual benefit, then, bringing her back to the Lord and also, most likely, to that lout of an absentee husband. To Mother too, perhaps. This thought made him angry. He could see her, the penitent sinner, meekly bearing the strokes of the old dragon's tyranny.

A little later Wendell was not so sure of this. He remembered the minutes after that night's event, the complacent look on her face and the way she shook her head when he asked if she was sorry. On a hot surge of his pulse he recalled those sexy groans and breath in his ear. "I hope you don't mean not to come back," he had called, watching the goodly shape of her body on the way out through the kitchen. Maybe, just maybe, in his absence she had indeed come back. Tapped at the door, maybe entered, calling softly to him. Between his ardent bouts of pacing from silent room to room he stood in a sort of trance at his upstairs window. He did not see her again.

At least he did not see her that afternoon and by dark his mind was deep once more in the real matter at hand. Two hours yet, not until ten. He was somewhere about his third cup of coffee when, like a gunshot, her footstep caused the cup to leap in his hand. He could not come up with so much as a word but Tricia did not need it. Opening the screen she stepped into the light and stood looking at him. It was a grave look, he did not know how to read it. He did know that his blood was coming back.

"I came to see you before," she finally said. "You were gone."

"Did you?" She had on those shorts.

"More than once. I thought maybe you were running away from me."

"I wouldn't do that. I didn't think you'd come back." The old blood was crowding his veins.

He sat looking at her, minding the yellow blouse her breast extended, that suited the tint of her flesh. "Sit down, I'll get you some coffee." But he did not remember to do so, watching her rather confidently take the chair at the end of the table. As if to keep them hidden from him she held her hands in her lap.

"Is everything all right?" he said at last, conscious only afterwards of his words. To give them point he nodded over his shoulder, toward her house. An oblique glance at the clock showed that it was only minutes after eight.

"I'm not afraid of her anymore." Her gaze on him, straight and bold, was like a confirmation.

To fill the pause he said, "Really?"

She nodded gravely. "Not anymore. I thought I would

be . . . after that, that night . . . more than ever. But I wasn't."

"No guilty feeling?" Wendell's throat felt tight.

"Just for a little while. Then it went away." Here she lowered her gaze to the tabletop. "Now I like to think about it when I'm with her. At first I felt like she might read my mind or something, but I got over that. Now I like to think about it right in front of her. When I'm giving her her shot, or anything."

"Not any other times? When you're not with her?" he managed.

She lifted her eyes and looked at him almost if not quite level. "Yes," she murmured.

Wendell had to draw a breath. The hands of the clock had moved a few minutes on but he could not simply spring at her. He tried to clear his head. "Does she see that, that you're not afraid of her?"

"I don't know. Maybe she does, she's more hateful than ever. And crazier."

In the pause his head had got clearer. "How, crazier?"

"Oh I told you. All that about drugs, that she gets out of the paper. And poor Mr. Farrow. It's getting like an obsession."

As clear as a bell he said, "How's it different?"

"Just more so. And she talks on the phone upstairs a lot. Long distance, I think. I've heard her say Mr. Farrow's name a lot of times. I don't know who she's talking to. Joe told her Mr. Farrow would sue her. I hope he does. I'd be glad if they put her in jail. I hate that old woman."

"You don't know who she's talking to?"

"I can't tell."

Wendell was quite cool now and for a long moment, thinking, he did not say anything. He would go to Farrow, tell him. But who would believe an old woman like her? He would go to Farrow anyway. "And Joe can't shut her up?"

"She won't listen him any more than anybody else. Joe's just a . . . But I don't want to talk about either one of them."

For what must have been a whole minute Wendell was barely even conscious that he was looking at her. He was thinking about Venutti, envisioning the swarthy face. A quiet little man, secretive. And the old woman's telephone calls? He looked at the clock.

"Are you sorry I came?" Tricia finally said, very softly.

"No. Of course I'm not." They knew what they were doing. They knew, if there was anything to know, about Venutti. A breath of air from the open door stirred in the kitchen.

"You look like you are."

Her hands were on the table, and round soft arms on which a down of hair was visible. An hour and a half.

"I'm not, though. I'm glad."

This was true again and feeling it get truer he said, "I'm real glad."

She seemed to be thinking about his words, weighing them. Then, just as if it was any casual question, she asked, "Do you want me?"

Wendell's response, once he had got her question fully digested, was only to say, "Let's go up to my room."

X

That night at the airstrip everything went off astonishingly as planned. In the three hours before the plane arrived, it seemed to Wendell that including those who put in an appearance and then left he saw at least twice as many people as he had thought were involved in the operation. Some of them were countersurveillance people on the way to their posts, and later he would hear their voices coming in over walkie-talkies. There was even one pair (he heard their voices on the big radio by the hangar door) stationed fifty miles away near Falls City to monitor the plane when it reached that point. Flashlights were still the only light, the nervous beams criss-crossing, lacing the night, suddenly calling faces out of the dark. Venutti's face was not one of them. But he might have been there, Wendell thought, and one of the voices, subdued for all their excitement, could have been Venutti's.

The excitement was no wonder. Here and there, listening in, he heard the talk. Seventeen thousand pounds, one dark face said, with a value of eight million anyway. And also coke, as Wendell later heard: another two or three million at the least. There was awe as well as excitement in the voices.

A little before two o'clock Wendell heard the plane, flying without lights, make a pass over the airstrip. He was at his particular job, in a pickup truck at the east end of the strip, and when he heard his code name Romeo I called over his walkie-talkie he switched the headlights on. Headlights at the other end instantly answered his and both rows of reflectors along the strip stood out like so many candles. There were other lights, beams across the sky, playing about up there in silence that lasted a minute or two. He heard the plane again. It flashed like a big bird out of the dark, leveling straight at him, gathering bulk as it came on. He was down full-length on the pickup seat when the plane's tires stopped screaming. Lifting his head he saw it, enormous, already making its slow and thunderous spin-around on the pavement.

It taxied back to the other end for unloading. Wendell was part of this, receiving the heavy bales from the cargo door and lifting them up to other hands that reached out from the van-trucks. There were only the flashlights now and low voices and one voice a little louder that kept urging them on, cursing them sometimes. It was quickly done. Maybe thirty minutes went by before the plane, all refueled and vacuumed out and manned with different pilots, passed like the boom of Judgment Day just over the top of his pickup. If there was anything miscalculated in the whole operation it was apparent only in the fact that daylight caught them still not quite through removing the reflectors. Otherwise no eye but a curious one would have spotted evidence of the night's activities.

At home Wendell slept through most of the day and for a change waked up with a head practically clear of any worries but one. This was the consideration that he did not yet have his money. But Hal had said three days. It would come to him. Five thousand dollars! And there under his mattress, like a surety for the rest, were the two thousand already his. He got out of bed as if this was to be the first step in his waiting.

But after all his head was not really clear of other worries. For a while he thought about narcs on the move, coming his way, about to surround the house with Venutti among them. He would have talked himself out of this small seizure all right if, on one of his glances out the windows, he had not happened to get a glimpse of Tricia. At first this simply arrested things: he stood there with a sense of trouble darkly defined. He thought of Mother and then, with a jolt, of her notions about Farrow. Those telephone calls! It was still an hour until dark. To help endure this hour he walked up-town to the Grill and, making it slow, ate his way through a hamburger.

He loitered over his coffee, ordered another cup, and loitered. That it was still daylight outside was like an inex-plicable perversity of the sun, a cosmic thwarting of his im-patience. The jukebox in the shadowy corner howled. Three men got up from a table and paid their bills and left and for a moment, facing the big wall mirror from his stool at the bar, he thought he was the only customer remaining. But there was another man.

Wendell did not know how he had failed to see him, be-cause the man's reflection in the glass, though shadowy, seemed as huge as it was sudden in Wendell's eyes. He had simply appeared, an apparition too big for the table where he sat eating, in what might have been watchful si-lence. Watching Wendell in the glass? There was not really light enough, yet Wendell thought he could make out the curious mottled yellow-brown of the eyes returning his gaze. Then, for a space, it was as if there was something down in Wendell's guts contorting, twisting and unbearable under his heart.

This was brief. Wendell knew, and in the moment of rec-ognition felt his blood go hot instead of cold. Hating the man, he thought of that tent meeting long ago, recalling the voice, the gestures, all the obscene terrors he had suffered by those ravings. Stupid. This was the face, the mold itself, of the troglodyte in its cave. He could have thrown his cup, his saucer, the heavy sugar bowl at it. All he did was step down off the bar stool and without a glance at the man pay his bill and go out into the street.

A few minutes walking in first twilight got his thoughts focused again. At the lot where the shiny tops of cars re-flected the afterglow he stopped to make sure there was no sign of life. It was almost late enough. Loitering, observing the few cars that passed by, he made his way back to Dan-ford's Corner and on toward Rudd Street.

Farrow was not there. The screech owl was there and the curtain of darkness up on the porch but no voice spoke. Even the light high up was not burning and when, uncertainly, he climbed the steps and knocked, all he could hear inside was a muted echo. What made him choose the steps to sit on was his uncomfortable sense of a presence there in the dark. His choice was no help. On the steps it was worse, and colder, and made the hair tingling at the back of his neck seem ready to stand up. Yet Farrow was not here. The owl fell silent. Farrow was not here, and at last getting up from the step Wendell went and confirmed it by the fact that the garage was empty. There by the garage was where he stayed and it must have been nearly midnight before he gave up and went home.

Wendell's distress kept harassing his sleep and when he waked up in full morning light he had a small idea. At least he might—mightn't he?—pump Tricia more on the subject. From his window the look of things was not encouraging. Tricia's car was gone and Joe's car stood in the drive. Only a little later he saw Joe, saw him on the gallery steps. He was helping Mother with great solicitude, and Wendell watched until he got her into the car and drove away. This gave him hope, for now the chances seemed good that Tricia, returning before they did, might be there alone. Wendell kept coming back to the window and after a couple of hours he saw her car, the only car.

His mistake was not unnatural. What must have happened was that in one of the intervals when he was not looking, both Tricia and Joe had returned and, with the old woman again installed in the house, had then driven away together. This was the cause of Wendell's mistake and he unnecessarily added a second mistake, a big one. He need only have tapped at the screen door, like a gentleman, before entering. But the screen wire blurred his vision and with his mind busy on what his questions would be he was sure that the person at the kitchen table was Tricia. So he walked right into something like the stare of a basilisk. What was he to say? What he fatuously came up with was "Excuse me."

The old eyes, for all their fallen color still scalpel sharp, did not excuse him. In fact they did not look as though they ever would excuse him, his being a young man who was not only no gentleman but maybe even something worse than a thief. Wendell had all but forgotten the set of this old woman's jaw and also, though she was sitting down, the height of her. Her walking stick, leaning against the table, was close to her hand. The thought crossed his mind that she might spring up and hit him with it.

"Do you always just walk into people's houses?"

He could not get hold of an answer. He did shake his head.

"What do you want?"

He started to say, Nothing. He actually said, just because it came to him, "I wanted to borrow a cup of sugar."

She looked at both his hands, in neither of which there was a cup.

"I forgot the cup," he said. "I'll go get it."

"No."

This stopped cold the movement he had not yet made.

"There's a cup." She meant the one on the counter beside the sink. "The sugar is in the canister there." After a moment she added, "Go get it."

So he had to, like acting in a charade. It was some comfort to have his back turned on her but not much: the weight of her gaze made his backbone stiff. Then it got worse. Pouring the sugar he saw that it was partly missing the cup. With his backbone now perfectly stiff he waited for her voice. When it came, though, it said, "Your name is Corbin, I believe you said?"

This was a great deal less than a help. He saw his old man, his mother, his brothers and sisters, all floating like so much garbage across her mind. He remembered his lie about being from Georgia, that Tricia had passed on to her, but somehow he knew it was no use, then or now. The old woman knew they were his, the Corbins of Bison Springs. His mouth made a sound like, "Yes ma'm."

As if to confirm his conclusion she said, "From down near Bison Springs, as I remember?"

He was about to say Yes ma'm again when something stopped his tongue. It was anger, the beginning of anger. He thought of the garbage floating across. "Yes," he said. He would not clean up the sugar.

"I thought that was your family."

He started to say Yes and then did say it, clearly. He even had the hardihood to glance over his shoulder at her. She was still watching him, if not with quite her former intensity.

"You have a brother named Fawbus," she said. "He's in the penitentiary, I believe. For selling drugs."

The shock was not because this was news to Wendell, which it was. What hit him was that *she* knew and, more, had made it a point to tell him. What for? His backbone went stiff all over again. What else did she know? He thought his best course was to say, "I haven't seen him in a long time."

"It was in the paper, some while back. You didn't know it?"

At the moment both Yes and No looked like losers and he only shook his head obscurely. There was a long pause with birds chattering out on the gallery. He thought about bolting.

"I suppose it's because you're an intellectual. I think intellectuals don't put much importance on family, do they?"

"I don't know," he mumbled. Should he bolt now? Or take up some posture? What posture? There was the spill of sugar on the counter, a problem. Then he felt, and a glance confirmed, that she was not even looking at him anymore.

"Of course, neither does anybody else now. You all have other concerns, that we never heard of when I was young. We couldn't have imagined a world without families. This whole little town was sort of like a family. You wouldn't believe that, to look at it now."

It was some relief, in this pause, to know that she was thinking about the town instead of him.

"I'm sure we were very provincial. We didn't have any intellectuals like Professor Rathbone. Nobody read that awful Hun my daughter-in-law is always reading in secret. We didn't have many secrets. What we did have was order, and manners, and some dignity. And people who were at least ashamed of selfish, ugly lives. If the Judge was still living . . . they would have to build more penitentiaries, I expect."

For himself, among the convicts? Wendell could see that she was looking hard at him again and he supposed, when it came, that he was what had produced her next reflection.

"But he's gone. And everybody like him. I think it's the devil who is in charge now. Along with his minions." She let Wendell digest this—pointedly, he thought. Suddenly, "I'll tell Patricia you dropped in."

She meant Go and Wendell started to turn. But the spilled sugar was there and when he moved she would see it.

"Don't forget your cup of sugar. I'll clean up the mess."

"Thank you," he mumbled. But he had taken only a couple of quick steps toward the door when she stopped him.

"Wait a minute." She had lifted a knotty old hand off the table. It settled slowly back while she sat just looking at him, face-on now. Forcing himself not to squirm Wendell waited for what was to come. She might have been trying, maybe with success, to read his mind.

"Do you know who Jason Farrow is?"

He thought, while she watched him, of No, then Yes and finally said, "No."

"He owns the car agency. He's even a councilman. And you've never heard of him?"

"I haven't been here very long. Just a couple of months." He did not think she believed him. He thought that what she wanted was to see him deny it.

"You must know there are drugs in this town, everybody does. Even schoolchildren get them. One died recently. Henry Farnsworth's boy."

"I don't know many people here." Then, on inspiration, "I spend most of my time studying and writing." Why did he think, just after speaking, that she had already dismissed this as a lie?

"And you've never heard talk about drugs? About who sells them?"

"No ma'm."

She did not *say* liar. She said, after a moment, "Please go on home," and turned her face away.

Not even thanking her again for the sugar Wendell went, and entered his own kitchen door as if the old woman was in pursuit. Then he was thinking that there were hours of daylight left and that he did not dare go looking for Farrow at the car lot. But a little later he did go. He stood across the street watching and saw only a couple of salesmen showing cars and Cat washing a car over behind the agency building. So, in the house again, spying from windows for a reason that no longer had to do with Tricia, he waited out the day.

It was somewhat better before night came on. The passage of hours had at least diluted his panic conviction that she not only had certain knowledge about Farrow but also knew of Wendell's connection with him. How could she? What had made him think that this old woman, any more than Farrow, could see into his mind, read his thoughts? Old bitch with her contempt. The thought of this, seeing himself like so much garbage in her eyes, made him writhe for a while—until he thought of Tricia on the sofa, on that bed under his naked body, with her groans. *There* was Mother's family, hot in his filthy Corbin grip. If she could have seen that in his mind—*there* was devil's work. For all his feverish distress here was a moment when a small grin of satisfaction came and spread his mouth.

It was full dark when Wendell stood among shrubs in Farrow's back yard and saw the light high up under the cupola. No voice spoke to him from the porch but he had already seen faint light in the back-door glass. It came from beyond the kitchen toward the front of the house and he lifted his hand and tremulously knocked. There was an interval without sound, not even the owl's cry. He saw Farrow in silhouette, a low neckless shape that in clear sober fact he never had seen before. That it was a comfort to see him this way, his shape defined and approaching the door like any man to open it, struck Wendell with a conviction of his own foolishness. If only he could have seen in detail the face that, after a moment, confronted him through the screen.

"Getting ready to send for you. Wait a minute."

Preparing words in his mind, Wendell stood there until Farrow came back with something in his hand. It was a paper sack, it was money. It was five thousand dollars, was it not? For a space, while his fingers tested the money inside the sack—incredible!—he forgot completely about the words ready in his mind.

"Set down." Farrow was back in his chair in the dark, without feature once more. Wendell did as told but even so, with this sack of money in hand, he could not get his mind clear again. Farrow said,

"Went off mighty good. Be more for you next time."

Next time? Wendell had not even thought about a next time and just for a moment this thought too obscured his urgency. "Another one like that?"

"Couple weeks. Maybe three."

Wendell's words came back. "You know that old woman, Mrs. Harker. You said she was making you trouble." When Farrow made no response he said, "She's been making phone calls. About you. Long distance. Her daughter-in-law told me. I saw her today . . . the old woman, I mean. She asked me about you, did I know who you are. And about drugs in town . . . who sells them. It's just a notion but she's crazy on it, getting crazier. Tricia says that."

Farrow was silent.

"I thought I ought to tell you. If she gets to making too much noise, you know, somebody might believe her, mightn't they? I was thinking maybe couldn't you threaten to sue her or something? That might . . ."

"I knowed her name was something like that," Farrow suddenly said. "Tricia, huh?"

"That's her daughter-in-law, that told me about her. I thought you ought to know it."

Just perceptibly Farrow moved in his chair. For the first time tonight Wendell heard the owl.

"I know it. Been knowing it. Know something about them phone calls, too." He paused. "Called Sheriff Budd, for one . . . just yesterday. He told me about it. That'd been all right, he belongs to me. Thing is, she made him tell her how to call up the Investigation Bureau." He fell silent again, briefly. "Trouble is, her husband was right big for a country judge and she still knows some people. So her being crazy don't guarantee us. I'm a careful man but it's nothing perfect."

A distressing interval ensued. Venutti came back to Wendell's mind.

"Naw. I been thinking. I been a good while thinking about it. Doing me some research, too. We need to put a hush on that old bitch."

Bitch was right. But how could he do it? Wendell murmured, "You don't think that might do, threatening to sue her?"

"Nah. Make her worse. Make too much noise anyhow."

What, then? Wendell had to wait a long time, hearing quite close by the owl's quavering voice. He had his money. He would take it and run.

"You're getting it from Miss Tricia, ain't you?"

Wendell's mouth came open in the dark. Cat's doing, spying on him. Goddamn his black soul.

"A gal like that ought to be a big help. Hates the old woman, don't she? Think about that."

Think about it? Wendell could only stare at the featureless shadow of him over there in the dark. Growing slowly under his skin was that cold sensation of being looked at out of a toad's face.

"Old woman a bad diabetic, getting her shots. More ailments besides. They tell me it's ways nobody'd notice. Natural-looking. A little mistake made, maybe. Think about that. Get you a book, you're a scholar."

It was as if Wendell's brain had shut down—or all but the parts that could register cold and a fluttering owl's cry.

"Let's let that be your next job. Need to rush it, too.

104

'Course I reckon we can afford some real money for this one. Twenty-five thousand seem about right?"

The figure without even stopping floated across Wendell's mind.

"Say twenty-five, then. On delivery. Need to make it soon, though. . . . You'll be the first rich man ever knowed in your family."

"You want me to . . . " This was all, his tongue stuck.

"Smart fellow like you'll work it out. That gal's your key. Might be, I'll have a little help for you, though." Then, "Better get on home and start on it."

Wendell was a long time understanding that he had been dismissed and then it seemed impossible to get up from his chair. He opened his mouth but nothing came out.

"It'll pleasure me anyhow," Farrow said. What he said next, after Wendell had finally got onto his feet, did not become perfectly clear in its meaning until Wendell remembered it later. "Cat'll be around. Cat and me both . . . if you need us."

XI

A sense of incredulity, of being enmeshed in circumstances that were not real, kept his thoughts not only unfocused but off in a kind of distance. Throughout that night he was waked from sleep by the stubborn certainty that he knew neither where he was nor how he had got here nor why. In the worst of these vertiginous moments it was necessary for him to start from scratch, with his family in the cabin on Mr. Cartwright's farm and trace his steps from there—through his career in Bison Springs, through college and graduate school, and finally to this place, this room where he lay in the dark. It defined a circle, or nearly so, for it seemed that he lay in shouting distance of the very ground on which he had sworn never again to set foot. He thought about Fate and how it was said to compel people's lives in spite of them.

This was a reflection he rejected but even so, in the dark of that disordered night, it appeared to have more substance than the realities circling like so many noiseless bats around his bed. Hit-man Wendell: the thought was like a glimpse of himself acting in a TV play. Wendell rich, counting his thousands, stuffing them under his mattress? Not this Wendell lying here, grown up from little Bubba. That was a dream Wendell, persisting still in a dream in which he had just come home from a toad's house. He was the outlaw Wendell, bribing a sheriff, patching an airstrip in the night, unloading bale after bale of grass from a giant airplane. Not this Wendell lying here innocent in his bed.

This state of mind, much more than his lucid intervals of desperation, was what he remembered best from his experience of that night. Half-conscious tricks of self-deception were common enough in times of stress and anguish and there was nothing remarkable in the fact that he, suddenly ensnared as he was, should react as others did. Even so, his case was special. That one night's practice somehow set a pattern that his mind, throughout the events that followed, kept resorting to. Without it, he later thought, he doubted whether he could have managed to do the things he did. He did them, as it were, partly outside of himself, half-thinking in a curious way that he was not really the culprit. There was this other Wendell, the true bastard, who stepped right across lines he balked at for his own self. If this was not always true, it was true enough of the time to give him some relief when he needed it most.

Wendell never did have physical evidence that he was being spied on. What he did have, based on Farrow's last words to him that night, was the conviction that this was true. Peeping out of windows and pausing to listen into the silence around him got to be habits. He would think he heard or glimpsed something at a window or even inside the house (Cat, he thought. Or somebody else?) but his alertness always failed to pay off. In those days he actually saw Cat only once: in the night of the second day when he came to Wendell's back door. But his mission now was not to spy.

"Just see how you making out," Cat said, fidgeting in the dim light from the kitchen bulb inside. The way he kept turning his head looked merely nervous until Wendell observed with a cold feeling that he was glancing toward Tricia's house. "Big Man want it, not me." His eyes that kept darting back to Wendell's face were green and not at all like a bird's. This was the moment of Wendell's first genuine feeling of revulsion toward Cat, a sort of spasm. Before he had quite recovered he saw that Cat's hand was extended. There was something in it, a small package.

"What's that?" Wendell barely got the words out of his throat. He thought he knew the kind of thing it was.

"He say this-here."

Wendell just looked at it.

"What he say." Then, "It's more stuff in there besides. Something wrote in there, too. He say look at it good. Say put it in your icebox."

Finally, reaching out, Wendell took the package.

He did not open it then. Putting it, hiding it deep behind dishes in the refrigerator he had in mind that maybe somehow he would fail to remember it was here.

Wendell's secret hoard became his consolation. Or diversion, rather, because diversion was what he used it for. He must have taken it from under his mattress a score of times each day and counted and recounted it, fingering every bill, studying each one's peculiar features. There were seven thousand dollars. He began to think about the things these dollars would buy and then to make and revise written lists of all the items, which he afterwards destroyed. This little game always ended in the same way, with visions of far places, dream places with a beach, maybe, and him at his ease on the sand. Of his former thoughts about flight only these remained.

Otherwise in these days he did not seem to have much control of his thoughts. Whenever his mind brought him up against that incredible business somewhere off in the future, they had a way of flying ascatter or retreating into irrelevancies. By fits and starts was a phrase that well described the way he went through the hours, expecting or dreading something. The clearest of his expectations was that Tricia would appear, but now he kept an eye out for her in the fear that she would do so—even in broad daylight, even with her husband's car parked there in the driveway. But there were also times when, suddenly and gratefully tumescent, he would sink from consciousness into a mirk of sensuous reverie. Such reveries came in his sleep too, but so did the chilling sensation of eyes watching him.

This paralysis—it was very like paralysis—lasted in its strength for most of three days. What broke or greatly weakened it was a plain shock of fear. The cause of the fear was no better than dubious but unlike all the little fears that had been dogging him, this one came in a single clarifying stroke. Moreover, it happened in the wake of what he later read as a meaningful preface to the event.

The telephone by the kitchen door had not rung once in many days. Now it did, with all the violence of an alarm, and when he picked it up no answering voice came. He heard breath but no voice, then the click. A wrong number, that was all, but there was no use telling himself this. He tried for an hour. The only result was that in a sort of desperation he did a thing he had been fearful of doing in these past days. He walked downtown. Later he felt that the voiceless telephone call was the significant cause of his impulse to do so.

Wendell rarely looked at a newspaper. Pausing, with groceries in hand, on Danford's Corner, in the watchful mood his outing had hardly diminished, he was waiting only for the traffic light to change. But a man walked past, an unfamiliar man who looked into his face. Wendell had the thought that this might be the caller and turning his head he saw the man stop, as if pointedly, and select a newspaper from one of the racks against the wall. It was like an exemplary act. Wendell bought the same paper and, keeping his normal stride, brought it home with him. He found the little story on page 3.

It need not have been Venutti. A body in a swamp in Upjohn County, stripped, unidentified. But the age was right and the color of the hair. A bullet, small caliber, in the back of the dark head. Wendell was sure. And the man who bought the paper, who was he? Wendell kept envisioning the way that man had looked into his face—a look with meaning in it. But even if all his conclusions were nothing more than the work of an overheated brain they were enough. From the not-forgotten hiding place in the refrigerator Wendell took out the package. This was a few minutes before sunset. When Tricia, as though in consequence of the day's events, came into the house that night she stood in the presence of a man who was no longer cloudy about his purpose.

His purpose itself was the one clear thing in Wendell's mind. This fact, an hour later in the still wake of their antics in his bed upstairs, descended on Wendell with a bemusing kind of clarity. There was a full moon, the room transformed in mellow shadow-light and the mirror over his mantel pure quicksilver. He listened to her breath, watching the rise and fall of her naked breasts tinted like old ivory in the gloam. Hushed breath, coming and going, no hint of that brazen shrillness in his ear. Suddenly it did not seem strange to think, for the first time, that these same breasts with nipples dark on the white must once in fact have suckled a baby. The heavy pause that held him suspended now issued at last in another kind of reflection. It came with a small uprush of gladness. For he knew that nothing within his power could ever bring this woman to the act he had in mind.

He did not think he had dozed. It had to be a cloudbank that abruptly made the mirror fail and at the same time called him back to the day's event. When he looked again Tricia was little more than a breathing shadow on the bed, but a shadow, as he soon made out, awake and looking at him. Thinking what? She answered his silent question.

"Do you want me again?"

"If you do," he finally said.

"Yes."

But no stirring of his blood followed. Rather, this Yes she had uttered stood there in the clarity of his mind like a word merely to be scrutinized. Letting lie the hand that came and settled on his arm, Wendell said what all of a sudden was given him to say.

"Is it me, or just to get back at Mother?"

He thought it was mostly the way he said it that made her after a moment remove her hand. But he knew now what his intention was. "Isn't it just her, because you hate her?"

"No it's not." But she said it hesitantly. She was really weighing the question. "I wouldn't do it with you if I didn't like you."

"But you hate her a lot more than you like me. You know you do. You hate her guts." She could not have seen how Wendell was straining to make out her face in the dark.

"That doesn't mean I don't like you. Because I do. A lot." After a time, in a voice nearly inaudible, she added, "Do you like me?"

"Yes," he said, or maybe only thought he said, because it breached a moment in which other words were being given to him. "I don't blame you for hating her. I guess she told you about me walking in on her the other day. I got a good look. I'd hate her worse than you do, in your shoes. What did she say about me? That I'm scum?"

Tricia hesitated. "She says that about everybody. Even if she doesn't say it she's thinking it."

Scum, he thought. But this was a pause that only sharpened his purpose. "And you've had that all these years. Waiting on her, putting up with it. How many more years?"

"I don't know." She drew a breath. "I've thought about leaving. Just walking out for good." Then, "But I wouldn't know where to go." Her voice receded. "I'm too old."

Wendell thought she was about to reach out to him again and he quickly said, "That wouldn't do, you'd lose everything. After all that." He drew a breath of his own. "Mightn't she die soon? Couldn't what she's got kill her anytime?"

"Some of them live on and on. She will too."

As if to shroud his design the darkness from that cloudbank persisted in the room. "You wish she would, though, don't you?"

A second passed. "Die, you mean?" But no words followed.

"You know you do. You're just afraid to say it. Why is it worse to say it than to think it?"

"I guess it's not." Then, "Yes, I wish she'd die."

"You ought to say what you think. Instead of hiding from

yourself." He pondered his next words carefully. "And *be* what you think. You're not somebody's trash to kick around. You've got a right to yourself."

She was thinking about this: he could tell she was gazing blankly up at the ceiling. She finally said, "I'm here, though. I never would have been, before. Before you came."

Wendell considered again. "Sneaking, though. Always sneaking. Hiding from that old . . . bitch."

"But I have to, you know I have to. What else could I do?"

"You could do yourself a favor." This came out before he was ready. Prudence stopped his tongue but not for long. He plunged again. "And everybody else. Her too." He did stop here, and waited. How could he throw it so baldly at her. Impossible.

"What favor?" she murmured.

He let go. "Sort of an accident. Natural-looking. The wrong kind of a shot, maybe."

In this long interval like a void he strained and strained to see her face. Then he was listening, trying to hear her breath. He heard it at last, followed ever so faintly by her words. "You mean . . . kill her?"

"If nobody knew. I could fix it . . ." His voice died off into another stillness.

"You don't mean that, do you?"

He said nothing.

"Do you?"

Still he said nothing. Mistake or not, he had gone too far.

"Why? Why do you hate her so much?"

"Because . . ." He had to think for a second. "Because I'm scum. It's for your sake, though, believe me."

Without one sound or motion in the room, two or three whole minutes must have passed. Out of the dark she murmured, "You really mean that?"

"Yes." For an instant he seemed to see her face.

"But I never could do that."

"I'd make it safe. A shot. Easy as pie." Then, "It's for you. I wish you'd think about it."

They lay there. Until moonlight bloomed in the room again Wendell could not be certain that her eyes were on him. They were, but not with an expression he could read in this light. Was it shock? It was as if he could hear his words sounding inside her head, and also in his own head words he had not spoken. There came a moment when he thought about trying to gloss it over, making a jest of it. Here the moonlight failed again and the room was in darkness.

A while later he thought about reaching out to her but he was too late. He watched her get up and palely fumbling in the dark put her clothes on and leave in silence. She would not come back. In later time Wendell would remember this particular moment well and how the thought had issued like a long sigh of reprieve from deep inside him. He would also remember that another thought had followed. It was the thought that once before she had left him in a silence all but identical to this one.

XII

He was a fool, she would not come back. But she would come back, because she had done so before. As by abrupt reversals of wind one thought canceled the other. In the afternoon of the second day he saw Tricia from his window. She stood with hands empty near the end of the gallery facing his way, looking or not looking up through the gap in the foliage to where he watched. What expression was on her face? Then she was gone, vanished into the house. She would not come back. He welcomed the fleeting sense of reprieve again.

Wendell never left the house. He paced and played the game with his money and endured even in sleep some watchful eye upon him.

On the third day he did one thing that was different. Included in the package from Farrow was an ounce or so of coke. He had never tried it before and after he did, one long acrid sniff, he knew as though from the inside out why it had been included. In making the dreams come easy it resembled pot but this was the end of the likeness. He felt none of that stunned or stony confinement in single moments of time. It was more like expansion in a sort of blazing clarity that put him in mind of second-sightedness. Things, objects, for all their lucid discreteness, joined together in patterns of meaning not visible before. It was a sense of possession, of total mastery that by an act of unriddling had stripped them of their stubborn mysteries. It was power, things were his. No backtalk, no problems for the future: easy enough, that matter that lay ahead. At his very highest moment he experienced a kind of certitude in himself that was like a briefly sustained bolt of illumination.

It was gentle in passing off: no afterwave of nausea or punishing rawness of nerves screwed tight. Yet there was something left over, a thing he perceived as a clouded after-image that off and on followed his consciousness about. Fastening on it he fancied that this was himself, the masterly undoubting self that he had become in that soaring interlude. The image was vaguely tenacious. It presented itself again the next morning and stood by him intermittently through the day. If it was not so vivid or compelling as something in a dream, it still was there like a presence to which he might be able to resort in a time of need.

A time of need came soon enough, that very afternoon, beginning when his first glimpse of her stopped him at a window. Tricia's garden, like his own, had gone unweeded for a while and he had no thought of seeing her there when his gaze passed over. But there she was and for an indefinite interval the sight of her, unbonneted in the hot sun, bent and stroking with her hoe, was the sole and only content of his mind. Yet he must have been thinking, because at the end of this interval he was sure he understood the reason for her being there. Wendell's decision, figured in the steps that took him so coolly deliberate down the stairs and out through the kitchen door, could not have been more lucid. At least it was as if that presence was instructing him.

For a time she did not see him watching her from the shade of the hedge. She saw the weeds, uprooted and falling beneath her hoe, and only the weeds—even when, where the corn rows stopped, her flushed sweat-streaming face was turned in Wendell's direction. She did hear his voice when he spoke, though at first she appeared not quite to know where it came from.

"You ought to get out of that sun."

She blinked at him. A lick of hair lay plastered on her forehead. She lifted a hand and with the back of it wiped the sweat from her eyes.

"Come on. In out of the sun."

She was looking at Wendell as if he was somebody doubtfully known to her. Or was it fear, distrust? She turned her eyes toward the house, her house. Through the screen of cedar trees not one window was visible.

"She can't see us. Come on."

"I can't." She shook her head once, then again.

"I've got some iced tea fixed."

Whatever she was about to say died in her mouth. He was the one who said something, something he could not clearly remember afterwards and that could not in itself have been persuasive. Yet, in the silent aftermath, the hoe handle slipped from her fingers and fell among the weeds.

Wendell would never know whether or not his evil little trick—the coke he slipped into her tea—had any effect, or whether such effect as it might have had was necessary. He did have the notion that she caught on, maybe even as early as when she took her first swallow from the glass. In any case she never reproached him with it. Probably, he thought, her bout with the weeds out there in the hot sun was a last effort at evasion in a four-day process whose result, when she let go of that hoe handle, was to put her in his hands. This, at the kitchen table as he sat coldly observing, was what her demeanor told him. It bespoke submission, a waiting for his instructions. But another thought, the dawn of a thought, came to his mind. It was one that he later saw to have been the critical, the devastating truth: that this submission had more to do with her feeling for him than with any other cause.

"What time do you have to tend to her?" Wendell asked.

For a second she looked startled, as though he had spoken roughly. The flush lingering in her face seemed not so much faded as it did diluted by a pallor underneath. "Before supper," she murmured. She looked up at the clock. It was not yet five.

"We could go upstairs."

"If you want to."

He barely heard her. "Finish your tea."

116

It was not that Wendell wanted her at this time. He did it because of what he seemed to understand now. This was the key. To have her groaning under him this ultimate time was all the turn it yet needed. In a cold way, imitating himself, drawing what lust he could from the noises in her throat, he managed the job all right. But there was an aftermath that was not all right. He noticed her eyes, an unexpected brightness there, suggesting all of a sudden that the first of his tricks also was working. Surely that had not been needed. He did not know why, at a time when his purpose never faltered, this thought should have brought so clear a pang of remorse.

This quickly passed. Words came and went across his mind, nothing stayed. She gazed at the ceiling, only that, and a long time while they lay in the gauzy flush of evening sun went by without any change. What did her empty gaze at the ceiling mean? Finally seizing the words he said, "She's probably waiting for you by now."

This got no response. In a dream, maybe, from the coke?— was this what her gaze reflected? "Let's get up," he said.

She looked at him. Instead of emptiness there was a question in her eyes. To stop it he said, "Come on," and got up from the bed.

The question never came. She did not speak as she dressed, and her actions made him think of somebody blind or in darkness. All wrong, it would not work. Uneasy, watching her over his shoulder as they descended, he led her into the kitchen. "Do you feel all right?"

Her nod, though it ended with face averted, was a little reassuring.

"Wait a minute." He took the syringe from the refrigerator and when he turned around he saw that her eyes were fastened on it. The eyes were clear.

"It's her shot," he said. "Just like always. Okay? Just give her her shot like always. It'll all be natural. Believe me." But she kept looking at it and finally he said, "Don't you believe me?"

"Yes."

"Let's go, then. I'll be with you every step."

But her eyes, trained on his face now, did not respond to his gesture. The clock behind him ticked, ticked. Her mouth said faintly, "Why?"

"You know why."

Another wasted gesture of his hand and he repeated, "You know why. All those things." He waited. Then words were on his tongue. "For me too . . . both of us. Believe me." Then, "I'll have to go on by myself if you won't."

After a second her eyes blinked. Not waiting he reached out and turned her gently toward the open door.

In Wendell's memory that brief passage—back and across to where the hedge gap opened into her garden, through and around to the narrow path between dense banks of boxwoods, then the garage, the house beyond—would come back almost step by step and take a long time to complete. There was something weighty and exhausting about it, like losing ground by the same steps that appeared to move them onward. A surprise to find, when they reached the gap, that they had got this far, and hard, impossible to think that moments more would see their feet on the steps to the gallery. He remembered a bird—a mockingbird, he thought, in one of the cedars—that sang with all the startling force of a bird perched on his shoulder.

Beyond the path, beside the garage, he reached and took her arm. "Mightn't she be in the kitchen? Go look."

She shook her head. But she went, walking slow as if the ground under her feet might fail, through spots of shade and slanted rays of the sun, along the walk and onto the gallery steps. Standing with the sunlight rich on her naked legs she waited awhile before she beckoned to him.

She was just inside when Wendell came up and softly drew open the screen door behind her. The red oilcloth on the table was set aglow from the west windows and seemed to be the focus of all her attention. Wendell whispered, "Are you sure she's up in her room?" He touched her. The look he got in response seemed uncomprehending.

118

"Are you all right?"

Her lips said Yes.

"Are you sure she's up there?"

"Yes," she whispered, audibly this time. Under one of her eyes was a smear of dirt. It had been there all along, he thought, but now it worried him. "Here." Taking her arm he drew her across to the sink. The box with the syringe was in his hand and, putting it on the counter, he picked up a cloth and wet it under the faucet. Like a child she held her face upturned while he wiped it clean, first the smear, then the rest of her face. He noticed now that it was dead pale, as if he had wiped the last of her color away. He took up the box and opened it. He put the syringe in her hand. "I'll be right behind you. Right outside the door."

She gazed at the syringe in her hand.

"Just like always." Then, "Do you understand?"

"Yes," she murmured. She looked up into his face and her lips moved as to shape a word that never did get spoken.

"Let's go." His hand on her arm he gently pushed and followed her into the hall.

She stopped only once, at the foot of the stairs, gazing up to the shadowy hall above. Holding back he let her have that moment. But this was not quite true, for in a different way it was his own moment. Through the wide doorway, in glazy late sunlight with its drifting motes, the living room presented itself. Reaching almost to the ceiling, with panes aglow, was the massive cabinet he remembered, the chandelier and gleaming mantelpiece, the dour portraits gazing down on the patterned circle of stiff unsittable chairs. Not empty, though, he suddenly imagined, thinking of people in those chairs, rigid ghosts staring at him. A Corbin in the house, at the foot of the stairs, with the Lady at his side. So his mind played with the fancy—until there was only Wendell bending to whisper in Tricia's ear. "Go on. I'm right behind you."

She did not look back again, even when she reached the top of the stairs and, turning past the newel post, left him standing there. The pattern of light near the back of the hall came from Mother's open door and Tricia, entering that light, paused just short of the threshold. Wendell saw her hand, clenched, lifted to the doorframe. No knock followed, nothing for a moment, while Tricia stood as if blind from the light in her face. Then Mother's voice, not uncourteously saying, "Come in, Patricia."

Staring at an empty doorway Wendell thought for a minute that the tumult of his own pulse might deafen him to any sound of voices. Then he heard one, Mother's. "Be careful, please," but he heard no answer. Mother's voice came again. "Are you sick, Patricia? You look so pale. You're trembling." Then, delayed, some inaudible words in a voice he would not have recognized. A sound of footsteps and he saw Tricia's silhouette in the doorway, stopped there, arrested by the commanding voice behind her. "Patricia, wait! Go lie down. I can get my own supper."

He thought that Tricia's answer maybe was that she would get it, herself. She was already moving when she spoke, approaching now at a rate that caused him when she reached the stairs to step aside out of her way. Later he would remember with great vividness just how, without pausing, she looked into his face as she passed by and how her lips moved without sound. Less swiftly for fear of betraying his presence he followed in her wake. When he reached the foot of the stairs she was out of sight.

She was in the kitchen. She was standing by the sink, just standing, the syringe in her trembling hand. He reached and took it from her, saw that it was empty. "You did it, didn't you?" he whispered. "Shot her with it?"

She did not look as though she had heard but her white mouth said, "Yes."

He saw that her head was cocked, and after that, for minutes anyway, the two of them stood listening together. Or trying to listen: that same mockingbird, as raucous as a jay, was busy in a shrub beside the gallery. Wendell heard, barely did:

"I have to fix her supper."

He thought about shaking his head but all he did was watch her turn and lift a trembling hand to the cabinet next to the sink.

At first he did not know what stopped her hand. The noise, a vivid thump, seemed to reach him only later, and after that there was the mockingbird's voice. Then Tricia's face, her white mouth telling him something he could not hear for a moment.

"I think she fell."

Yes, Wendell thought and kept thinking until in sudden clarity he reached and closed his hand on Tricia's arm. It was to stop her. "Wait a little longer. It's too late anyway."

For a moment she struggled against his hand, subsiding into stillness. This was how they stood, kept standing, through the long space until the shadows gathered.

XIII

If Wendell had really seen, up close and in daylight, the old woman lying dead on the floor he might not have been able to maintain the degree of detachment that kept his thoughts as clear as they were. Even Tricia's halting words on the telephone, delivered out of a face spectral white in the dusk, were not unlike words heard from a distance, lacking the resonance needed to make them real. Vaguely like a play, was how he at first recalled that interlude; or like a scene he could have imagined when working on his novel. This was the state of mind in which he managed the sequel that night, and ahead of the arriving ambulance took himself offstage and into the dark.

For a while it was the state of mind in which from his dark window he watched additional lights come on and cars arrive and people approach and leave the house. Soon, though, it began to fail him. The change at first was a kind of distress, as though a protective shell around him had fissures growing in it. He reached for the empty syringe in his pocket, and found it. Safe. His next thought, that took some moments to clarify itself, was like a seizure. Tricia fallen hysterical, spilling it, screaming it out, and faces listening gravely and turning to look his way. Wendell, his breath stopped, drew back from the window.

But only occasional muted voices ruffled the quiet night. Until, on the gallery steps, a figure appeared and, hurrying to a car, backed out and drove away. Why the hurry? Headed where? Only a little after this was when the thought of an autopsy erupted into Wendell's mind. He moved to his bed but he did not stay there long. He was on his feet on the way to Farrow's house.

He got as far as the hall outside his room. Not yet, not now, when he might be seen abroad. Back at the window with fear in his throat he set himself to wait at least until the lights went out.

He did not go at all that night. It was because he remembered the coke, and after that he watched with a different kind of intentness, without fear, with a certain lust to see. The same foreknowingness came back and when he saw the lights go out and heard the stillness spread itself where the murmur of voices had been it was oddly like observing events his will had caused to happen. High up and unreachable in his room he made a light of his own and stood there content in the blaze of it. Remembering, he fetched his money out. There was more, much more to come. He counted even that, multiplying the numbers, watching his accomplished hands place bill on top of bill. The accomplished hands were his, and he was Wendell Corbin.

Sleep came unbidden and profound, and daylight waked him to a sense of troubles all but passed away. It was as if a residual something from last night's indulgence, a certain detachment and clarity, still abided with him. If there were real fears waiting out there they would not stir him to panic, and when, still in his bed, he observed that even at this late hour nothing had happened, no knock at his door, he arose with new assurance. He took more assurance still from the view across the hedge. Things were as they should be— parked cars in the driveway and the street, the hush unbroken. Later with only small misgivings he walked to the Grill and ate most of the breakfast he bought. There was some talk behind him in the room but nothing to the point that he could hear. And out in the street the cars and trucks passed by and people moved serenely along the sidewalks.

The persistent anxiety that dogged Wendell into the afternoon was his thought about an autopsy. Around two o'clock even this paled away to a shadow. The hearse arrived. He watched the black coffin until its bearers took it out of sight beyond the front corner of the house. He was safe, he thought, figuring the time elapsed and how, if *that* had happened, this arrival surely was too soon. Nothing at all had happened. There was only the sunlit hush and birds singing in it.

What came to Wendell then was not just a feeling of release. It had about it a sense of well-being different only in degree from what he had felt in some of his moments last night. Unreachable was the word, and it shaped the mood that an hour later became the cause of a decision he would not have taken otherwise. This was not the cause he cited when making up his mind: he had a prudential reason. He was only doing, compelled for appearance' sake, a thing expected of any next-door neighbor.

Reckless. On the walkway to Tricia's front porch this thought came starkly to mind, he started to turn back. But he was seen, it was too late: a woman stood at the open door. It was not Tricia, he could see that. But what if he met her face-to-face inside? Fool! He mounted the steps between the slim white columns.

Wendell did not see her, either in the living room, where faces had turned his way, or to his right in the parlor, where the coffin was visible. He muttered his name, some other words. A cousin, the woman said she was, with a name that passed him by. "So sweet of you. They're so broken up, you know." And then, "Won't you come view her? She looks so beautiful."

View her? Somewhere back in the shades of Wendell's mind was the thought that this was what he had come for. Not now, not yet. He felt the blood draining from his face.

"In here," the woman's soft voice said. No was almost his answer.

But there was no help for it. The woman steered him by his arm.

There was such a scent of flowers, banks and banks of them, rankly sweet in his nostrils and hard to breathe. Raised

124

a little above the coffin's rim was the face, with eyelids shut. Around it on the pillow, now that he could see, the white white hair was like a nest in which her head reclined.

"You can see how beautiful she was," the woman said, murmuring. "Look at her hands. Such lovely hands."

Long hands made of wax, it seemed, with tapered fingers lying vaguely clasped. He had no memory of the hands. Or the face either, now that he looked again, fastened his gaze on it. The mouth? He tried to remember, ceased to try. Hovering at the edge of his consciousness was the half-shaped thought that there was some mistake.

"Excuse me, please." It was the woman, leaving him there, already passing through the door.

It seemed to Wendell then, and continued afterwards to seem so, that what happened next was not in fact accidental—as though something discrete from his mind's confusion propelled him straightaway into an encounter of its own making. It came like a blow in darkness, in the same second that he, leaving the riddle of the dead face behind him, set a retreating foot in the doorway to the hall.

Beyond the woman, towering head and shoulders above her, stood that preacher he remembered with such hatred. This in itself would have been enough. But the man's eyes, that appeared to Wendell an almost feral yellow, looked, kept looking, straight into his face. This may have lasted mere seconds maybe, Wendell could not tell. Stopped on the threshold, in a kind of helpless submission to the eyes, he could only know that his inmost thoughts stood bleakly revealed in his face. So it seemed to him then, beyond any question. He thought afterwards that it was only the woman who, by taking the man's arm as she had taken Wendell's, delivered him from a consequence impossible to envision.

That had been hours now, hours in which the pain at his temples never missed a beat. Minutes more and fresh night air in the streets would soothe it away. But this image would not take hold. He was back in that helpless moment, visible to himself, framed in the door with her dead face behind him. And his own face, Wendell's. He tried to see it better. He stood in front of the mirror but the light was almost gone. His reflection was a shadow, with shadow eyes and mouth.

Nearly dark. In the murk of their foolishness again his fears seemed barely specters. Could a face reveal such things? Stupid fears. He went downstairs and stood at the back door waiting. Had the man seen his confusion beside the coffin? It was the same old woman, of course . . . only changed by death. Dark now. He closed the screen door softly behind him.

There were children playing in the alley. Concealed among shrubbery at the corner he watched by glimpses their shadow-shapes chasing back and forth. Flickering past, at hide-and-seek, fragmenting the quiet night with shrieks and laughter. It went on a long time, until he felt pain from the way his teeth were clenched. But something else came on him, something without a hint of preparation, like sleep falling. The children's cries grew distant and came from so far away that there was no telling about their direction. He seemed to know this much: they came from a place where he once had been and wanted above all things to be again. Then there was silence. A minute later he stepped out into the empty alley.

That night gave Wendell his first close look at Farrow. Instead of back onto the porch he was led through the dark kitchen to a lighted room that might have been a parlor once. Lighted but not well lighted. A hooded lamp burned on the desk and except for this one pool of illumination cast no more than a greenish shadow on the stark plaster walls. Nothing on those walls, not unless one counted a curtain that hid a single window. The furniture, the scarred desk and two stiff armless chairs, had the look of items abandoned on purpose at the end of an exodus. On the chair nearest the door Wendell sat facing him.

He had not even known that Farrow wore glasses. They were tinted glasses, obscuring the eyes that surely were observing Wendell. If this was a small distress it did not last long, not in light that at least was enough this time and revealed a man like any other—a thickset man of middle years, with rounded shoulders and not much neck and thin hair going gray. His hands lay on his knees, his fingers tipped with blunt but polished nails. No doubt some trouble with his eyes required these tinted glasses in the light. Except for the bodily stillness peculiar to him, nothing recalled the figure so darkly familiar in Wendell's mind.

But these in such detail were observations he was to make later. Not at first when, tense in his chair, he tried for words that would not get straight in his mouth. It was Farrow, finally, who ended the silence.

"Bothering you, huh?"

"I'm afraid it is," Wendell said, not quite audibly.

"Done with now. Few days, a week, you'll be all right. Put it behind you, you're safe. Think about your money."

The thought flickered across his mind. He forced his clenched hands open. "I might have made a mistake."

What followed was the one moment in the conversation when his old impression of Farrow seized on his mind again. Farrow had been still before this but not in the way he was now, with his gaze through the smoky lenses somehow visibly fixed on Wendell. It was as if a draft had got into the room.

"What mistake?"

Wendell swallowed. "I don't think I should have gone over there. To her house, this afternoon. To pay respects. Because I live next door. I thought . . ."

Farrow was waiting, watching from the darkness behind his lenses.

"I got upset, nervous. There was this preacher I remember, from way back. It's the way he watched me . . . while I was looking at the body, I think, and right afterwards. Like some way he knew what I was thinking."

"What way?"

"I don't know. A gut feeling. I don't even really know him. I saw him another time, a week or two ago. He was watching me then too. Like he knew something."

"You didn't say nothing?"

"No. But I kind of panicked. I left too quick."

The hidden gaze was surely studying him. "You didn't slip up nowhere else? No-time?"

He tried to think. He shook his head.

"You sure? Brought that needle away with you?"

"Yes," he breathed.

"And didn't leave no signs of yourself?"

"No, I was careful." Then the thought came back full-blown, both thoughts. "What if they did an autopsy? And Tricia, I worry about her . . . breaking down or something."

Farrow moved, though only his head, and allowed some seconds to pass. "Ain't nobody come for you, have they? Naw. Wasn't no autopsy. Won't be. Wouldn't show nothing anyhow, like I told you in my note. Little Tricia be all right. Woman like her ain't going to put any rope around her neck. Naw, you can rest easy. Start thinking about how rich you've got. Day or two, I'll have that money for you."

A day or two. It would come. Money as real as what he had now that his hands were always counting. And then? A distant place without definition stood in his mind for a second. Then he was envisioning the old woman's dead face.

"You'll be fine. Just get your mind right. And don't worry about no preacher looking at you."

"I don't even know what his name is." This slipped out: he wished it had not. It made another silence that he ended by saying, "It doesn't matter."

"Naw. It don't. I knowed some preachers when I was a boy . . . and a fool. One of them turned my head for a while. Had me worrying about my sins. Couldn't sleep for worrying about the devil getting my soul. Which was something they had me thinking I had, back then. It didn't last long, though." Farrow paused. "Naw. It didn't take me long. There's two kinds in the world. There's some that's willing to see what their eyes show them, and all the rest that ain't. I wasn't born the kind to make it up to suit me. Naw. If there was such a thing as a devil he'd be the one to say your prayers to."

It was not the words so much as the voice, grown intimate and curiously resonant, that was a comfort to Wendell.

128

"Just follow your eyes, boy, it's all in the seeing. And clean them made-up notions out of your head. All them church-going words, they don't mean a thing more than the wind blowing. You done just exactly the same as everybody else does: what it was give you to do. And calling it a bad name don't change it one bit. Not if you're a man, it don't, a man thinks for hisself. But you know that already."

He believed he said Yes aloud: to answer required an effort like breaking out of a stare. It seemed that Farrow, chair and all, had moved closer. But this was because instead of sitting upright he now leaned forward toward Wendell. His wide mouth was parted to speak.

"Naw, Wendell, I studied you good. We come out of the same old hopper, me and you. Down there where the trash is all at and life ain't nothing much but getting dumped on. Looking up at them, dodging it. Except that's how we got one-up on them, seeing their bottomsides when they didn't know we was looking. But we was looking, and ain't forgot a thing. That was your real education, my boy."

XIV

Although Wendell left Farrow's house feeling much easier in his mind he still had some days to go before he began to think of that night as a culminating point. Then he saw it as the decisive event in his personal history, when he became the Wendell Corbin he was destined to be. That visit was a threshold he had crossed and each day since a farther step to final confirmation.

They were not untroubled days. There were times, some of them lasting for hours, when fear and doubt stood knotted in his throat. A question would come down hard among his thoughts, and sounds of knocking or voices at his door would take violent hold of his imagination. But these seizures grew less, ending nearly always in a heady sense of deliverance. Even on the first day, there was one such ending.

From his window he saw the funeral begin, the coffin carried to the hearse and Tricia, in dark hat and veil, accompanied by husband and son, get into the waiting limousine. Then the departure, the last in the procession of cars vanishing down the street. After that came stillness. But suddenly it was not the old stillness. To Wendell's mind the faint birdsongs beginning now to puncture it were those of new and different birds.

And there was the night when, with something obscurely leaden against his heart, he received the money from Farrow on the dark porch.

"You got a good place for it?"

"Under my mattress upstairs. There's nobody else in the house."

"Get you some place better."

He did, under the house in a recess where a stone was dislodged from a stanchion. But this was later, after the counting and counting again in the light of the lamp by his bed. It was not to be believed! Thousands, tens of thousands, in stacks on the bed beside him. Wendell rich, spitting-rich, so rich that nothing could touch him. He came to remember that interval as something bracketed. In the glow under his lamp, there was not one fear to shadow him.

Inflated though it was, that hour anticipated the Wendell taking shape. A few more days achieved him. At least, in his new confidence, that was how it seemed. Late in the night a drenching shower came on, with whole trees of lightning standing in the west and stunning blasts of thunder that rattled the windows. When he waked up again it had made a difference in things—the air, the vivid light, the foliage washed new green in the morning sun. But the real differ-ence was in him. Standing naked at his window he felt as though he had just now shed the last dried-out integuments of the Wendell that used to be.

Except for the one glimpse of her getting into the limou-sine he had not set eyes on Tricia since that night. But on this bright morning, there she was, as cheerfully dressed as any wife going somewhere with her husband. He watched them get into Joe's car and drive away, leaving a house that stood all radiant white in the morning sun—an empty house. The empty room upstairs came back to mind. What had made the emptiness was vivid enough in memory, but vivid with a difference. He was able now, if not yet without a tightening in his chest, to look back on it as on a memorable event al-ready receding into the past.

This was the Wendell finally brought to birth. He was somebody new, and the confirmation was the sense he had of existing in a separate, secret world, invisible beneath the disguise that was his former self. He would remember well, from that same bright day, his walk downtown to the Grill. By now there were many familiar faces and here and there a nod of recognition. Except it was not recognition. He would think this and, nodding back, experience a feeling that he could describe only as partaking of both elation and contempt. What did such people know? Louts and drudges trained only to see themselves repeated in him.

Thinking this, on his bar stool in the Grill, he watched their busy reflections in the mirror—stuffing their blank faces, falling to with fat or lean jaws pumping, rounding on their food. Feeding time with human voices instead of grunts at a trough. Putting the last of his sandwich down he paid his bill and left.

It could have been that many such days alone with himself would have undermined this state of his soul. Whether or not, there was no such trial. It struck Wendell exactly right when on the night of this same day he received by telephone directions different from any previous ones. They appeared to mean—rightly, as it turned out—an airplane flight, and this expectation filled his night's sleep with dreams of his weightless body soaring across an unclouded sky.

Before the appointed hour of nine he was at the Atlanta airport, at a table well back in the twilight of a bar yet uninhabited by customers. The man, small, with a small hooked predator's nose, entered and put a suitcase by Wendell's side before he seated himself. It was simple. Wendell was to be the laundry man for the money packed in the suitcase. At Grand Cayman Island, Georgetown, where a man named Ramirez would meet him. A ticket and also a wallet were handed to him. He was sitting there alone when the first drops of sweat began to leak from his armpits.

But there was no challenge, no trouble. On the plane he put the suitcase under his seat and sat holding it locked between his heels. Then up, higher and higher above a world shrinking under his eyes, grown harmless now. When the stewardess came to his seat he ordered whiskey.

The glow from that drink and then another stayed with him throughout the day and the whole long night that followed. There was his business, astonishingly easy in the nut-colored hands of Mr. Ramirez, who smiled him welcome with perfect teeth under a mustache like a pencil line. They drove, a few minutes' drive in a topless sports car, through light whiter than Wendell had ever seen and azure glimpses of the ocean and trees he knew for coconut palms riffled high up by the wind, into a town where certain streets were pictures from a postcard. The bank among shops in a noisy street gleamed in that white light.

Twenty minutes accomplished it all. In an office plush with leather and polished glass he watched the money, amazing money, counted. He listened to Mr. Ramirez and put to documents the name already given him. In the end he was holding cashier's checks in amounts to make a man's hair stand up. After that his time was his. If there in the bank he did experience some starts of uneasiness, the white light of the sun outside quite blinded his memory of them.

There was the dazzling beach, tremulous miles of it, defined in softer mellow light as the sun moved on toward evening. He bought a swim suit and walked, his steps a glassy sound, and in the sea, beyond the surf, let the billows lift and float his body back to shore. Among the white buildings along the beach were bars as cool and dim as caves inside. There were sweet rum drinks and a kind of music that might as well have been brand new to him and more bare flesh of girls and women than his distracted gaze could keep in focus. And there was his hotel, rambling among palm trees, where black bellhops with clicking heels smiled like courtiers eager in his service. A prince. Wendell ceased even to count the money he put in hands.

He had to go back tomorrow, back to his room. This thought kept shadowing him, but later on, unexpectedly, it ceased to present itself in the gray light of depression. He had a steady flame in his head from all the drinks and sun-browned girls and music in the bars, but this was not really the cause. What he now could see with a clarity quite new was his remoteness from the old Wendell cowering in his room. What did that self matter here, a thousand miles away? A discarded self, a sweaty memory. He recalled his dreams of far-off places, so many self-deceptions. But here the dreams were made real and before too long, free of that old self, he would come back with his money to live among them. This was the recognition that put a new light on tomorrow.

There was a particular rum drink, a cuba libre, that he settled on that night and kept lifting, each time a little higher, in silent toast to his freedom. His final toast occurred in a bar now indistinguishable from the half-dozen previous ones he had inhabited. The music came from a band at the back of the room, amplified by walls that looked like coral. Even at this hour the place was a screaming tangle of motion and flickering light and contending voices that put him in mind of riot at the brink. Mostly it went on around him, though, while he sat in his own quiet at the bar, sometimes watching his dim reflection in the mirror opposite. Off and on he imagined that the dimness concealed unfamiliar features and that more light would show him a face requiring a different name. What name? None presented itself but he lifted anyway a now-empty glass to the reflection and saw, just barely, the obscure smile his face gave back.

This gesture of Wendell's was the cause of what happened next. On the barstool beside him was a lean blond man with a blistered neck and hands that were alternately busy pouring beer into his glass and pawing a girl on the other side of him. Until now Wendell had paid only attention enough to notice these things and that the girl, with mulatto-colored skin, was attractive and for sale. But now the man had made a comment about him. Wendell heard it late, on the way back, as it were, in a British accent. "Rather an empty toast, I'd say. Made the fellow smile, though."

Wendell did not afterwards recall that the remark produced in him anything more than mild vexation. In fact the decision he reached might have been the result of a perfectly cool inquiry put to himself. In a tone not even slightly vexed he said, "You better keep your mind on your slut, there."

He was looking into sunburnt eyes. He saw them change, a small contraction, and it suddenly occurred to him what a target the side of the man's head, a bit higher than his own, would make for his right hand. This time it seemed to be the music, a startling shriek of some instrument, that thrust the decision forward in his mind. But his hand changed its intention along the way. It closed on the neck of the man's beer bottle and accelerating struck the recoiling head just over the eye. The man fell backward off the stool. Wendell stood with a shard of bottle extending from his fist and contemplated a supine British subject lying coldcocked with a runnel of blood pooling on the floor beside his head.

Something like silence had fallen but it was the girl that put the alarm in Wendell's mind. He saw her hustling at a sort of trot toward the door and it came to him that he had better follow suit. He did, and quickly, with a couple of shouts pursuing him. But there was no other kind of pursuit and, taking the first corner into a street entirely deserted, he soon slowed to a walk. Later he worried—needlessly, as it turned out—but at the time he was more concerned with the thought that now this night was over.

It was not over. As it developed, the girl from the bar had taken the same turn he had taken. She was ahead of him passing through the aura from one of the half-lit shops, a glimpse that abruptly summoned his dwindling pulse. It seemed as though she knew at once whose steps were gaining on her and, clearly frightened, she led him something of a chase for another block or two. He remembered enjoying that, seeing the gap between them close, seeing himself in the role of pursuer along the empty street. It was the same way when he caught her, beside a little park where there was a wall and a palm tree with fronds rattling in the breeze over their heads. She was short and looking down into her face he gave her a few seconds in which to consider her situation.

In fact, throughout the hour or so before he left her room in first daylight, this was the way he kept it between them. Except that her face was pretty and with few interruptions wore the same furtively anxious expression, he left there with no distinct memories of her person. He himself was the one he remembered, as though he had used her services mainly to see what he would do. His performance did have its differences. There were things he put her to, twists he had nowhere known before except in the heat of daydreams. But the main thing different was that expression he caused her to keep on her face. This really was a new kind of pleasure, and its one decisive interruption, when she gave him the quavering smile, was not in fact an interruption. At the end, when he was dressed, he said, "How much do you get?"

She was afraid. In a voice that all but made a question of it she said, "Ten dollar be okay."

He put a hundred dollars on the table and departed her sorry room.

Wendell was met at the Atlanta airport by the same small man and before suppertime he was back in his room. That it held no welcome for him was hardly unexpected: the lapse of spirit he suffered was bound to come. So he was grateful when a timely anonymous voice on the phone issued another summons. It meant that *next time* had arrived. In the hours remaining before his departure he found it no longer so hard to ignore the view from his upstairs window.

That night at still another motel he was among people of whom about half were new to him. The new ones seemed to be from other and distant locations where The Company, always growing, had branches just like this one. But Hal was still on the scene, as redneck gaudy as ever, with his tiepin that said HOPE. Wendell did not see Calvin Walls but McCauley was present, world-wearily lounging on the bed farthest from the door. And Wendell was there, differently there, without any thought of bolting.

If most of the chores that fell to Wendell's hands were the same as before, the hands were not. Sealing that sheriff's mouth was again his business but he accomplished it this time like the somebody else he was, without a tremor. It hap-

136

pened on a logging road three miles from Appleton. The sheriff wanted double, beyond Wendell's limit. "Too chancy for chicken feed. Too many snoopers. Anyhow, our new church building has done run over the estimate. It's the Lord's work calling."

"Well, He'll have to settle for five. That's our top. There's other places."

Sheriff Grissom pursed his mouth and Wendell could see a shrewd look replacing the benevolent one. He quickly said, "It's too late now. You're in too deep to start thinking."

The sheriff looked up at the trees and Wendell watched his expression transform itself into one of resignation.

"Well, the Lord's will. Just say . . . five."

One different kind of assignment was fetching a truck, a big van, all the way from Mobile and turning it over to a man called Pedro just off the interstate south of Montgomery. Then to Atlanta, for gas bladders this time, and also to Birmingham to pick up the two pilots who were to replace the old ones when the plane landed. All smooth, no hitch anywhere, including the night of the big event when Wendell again sat waiting for the plane to show. In a way it was like his own personal doing when he saw it, just after one o'clock, flash into the aura of light and loom gigantically toward him down the strip. There was a fortune in that plane and some of this too was his.

XV

Somebody had made his bed and straightened his room. This was the matter tugging at Wendell's mind when just before sunset he came drifting out of his long day's sleep. The counterpane stretched tight, books and papers in order on his table. So it had been in first daylight this morning, a small wonder afloat in the haze of his exhaustion. It was still a wonder now—until he got his mind's eye focused.

Of course: who else? He lay thinking about it, seeing her enter at the back door, stop there for a time and then, passing through to the front hall, mount the stairs to his room. A mess. At last she quietly entered and went about setting things straight. Maybe more than once: she might have come other times in these past days. Maybe, leaning to make his bed, she had lain down on it, wanting him. The stab of his lust was one thing with the thought.

Then the thought was gone. It was all too easy to read what these signs meant. Thinking about this, Wendell put on his clothes and went downstairs to the kitchen. Here it was worse. Dishes long stacked in the sink had been washed and neatly put away. All spruce, set in order, even the sorry array of silver polished. He stood for a baleful minute or two and noticed, finally, that dusk was coming on. Hurrying he walked downtown to the Grill and sat for a long time after he finished eating. Was there any compelling reason for him to go on living in that house?

After seeing a movie at the tiny theater in town he walked home along the quiet street. He could see no light in Tricia's house—only the house standing bone-white and tall in rays of the moon. Was she there? What were her habits now . . . and Joe's? Relieved that he could not see any car as he passed by, he went to his room and sat blankly on the bed. Later he went out and warily checked on his money under the house. In need of something he took his old dead manuscript out of the drawer and sat at his table trying to read it. It seemed, as he pushed on, that even the handwriting was strange to him.

Wendell had not heard a car come into the driveway over there or any sound before the dubious one that made him lift his eyes. Why had he not locked the back door? The sound, identifiable now, was footsteps from out on the stairs. He had to wait a while, hearing the steps approach without assurance. She stood at his door.

She just stood, in half-light that made it uncertain whether she was looking directly at him, in a skirt now and maybe the yellow blouse he remembered. He cast about for something to say and came out with, "You cleaned up, didn't you?"

"A little."

He barely heard. She went on standing there and finally he said, "What for?"

"It needed it so bad."

He stifled an irritable reply and against his impulse said, "Come on in."

Wendell was taken aback. Where she had sat down, in the only other chair, put her face in the direct light of his lamp. Just for an instant he was struck with the thought that it was a different face, though different in a way that escaped him. It was her expression, he thought next, as if in a moment of mild alarm it had got set this way, with eyes held a little too wide open to be natural. He was accustomed to her lipstick but not this kind, accenting her mouth like flame against the general pallor of her face. She sat regarding him with a muted agitation plainest in the tenseness of her hands and in the moments when her gaze fled from his own uncertain one. To stop the silence growing too heavy between them Wendell said, "Joe's off on a trip again, I guess."

She nodded.

"Little Joe gone too?"

"He went back to Florida."

The silence again, growing too big, the whole house full of it. "You're all by yourself, then, over there?"

"Yes."

She was waiting. She was waiting for him to bring it up. Abruptly it came on him to say, "I've been looking at a new job, away from here. That's why I've been gone so much. I might have to move away."

Her wide eyes were fixed on him. But nothing more, no movement, in silence like a density pressing upon his nerves. Just slightly her bright lips parted and stayed that way until finally she murmured, "Away from here?"

"I might have to. I think."

"Clear away? From Turnbull?"

Her voice was barely not a whisper and this was when, with growing uneasiness, he observed a change in her face. She might have been looking at him from the dazed aftermath of a physical blow.

"Not yet, though," he quickly said. "It would be awhile." But it would be soon. Another still moment passed.

"Please don't." This was a whisper, more a movement of lips than a sound.

"Maybe I won't," he said. "It would be a long time, anyway." But it could be tomorrow, maybe, or the next day.

"I couldn't stand it . . . by myself."

Wendell stopped looking at her. He even tried turning his mind elsewhere, listening with a curious discomfort to the song of a mockingbird out in the moonlight.

"I keep hearing her upstairs. Sometimes I think I hear her calling me. Just as plain."

After a moment, setting himself, he said, "That'll stop. It'll go away pretty soon. People are always hearing that kind of thing." He gazed at the meaningless words on the page under his eyes—squiggles in a strange hand.

"But it's worse when Joe's at home, another way. When he looks at me . . ."

"He doesn't see anything different," Wendell said. And then, "Not if you'd wipe off that goddamn lipstick, it doesn't fit." He did not know how this vexation, rising toward anger, had slipped up on him. He saw her pinch her lips together, to hide the stuff. "That's bound to catch his eye. Do you wear that in front of him?"

The tentative way she shook her head expressed more of confusion than denial.

"Look," he said. "You've done plenty, with me, and he never saw it in your face, did he? He can't see this either. It's all over with and nobody knows anything about it. Nothing, not even a suspicion. . . . And I don't think God's going to do anything. Is that what's the matter, God'll get you?"

If she was not looking at him she was listening.

"You don't believe in that Sunday school shit any more than I do. If you stop being scared it'll go away. Think about being your own woman now. If you've got to think about her, think about the lousy way she did you all those years. You're not her trash anymore." A gust of real anger gave edge to the voice in which he suddenly added, "Go back to reading your Nietzsche. If he wasn't just something for you to tease yourself with."

He could not know that she felt this, she had let her head droop. He knew that he was not sorry, and it was an instinctive caution that made him curb his tongue and sit waiting for her to speak again. She finally did, with her head still bowed.

"It's just I can't . . ."

"What?"

"Stop feeling, you know . . ."

"Wicked? Well, go ahead and wallow in it if you've got to. Just be sure to keep your mouth shut, good and tight. You'll get enough of it pretty soon." He got up from his chair and stepped to the window. In some tree out there that bird was still carrying on with its uncomfortable song. But the silence behind him soon got the best of it. He heard her voice.

"Just don't go yet. Not for a while."

At first he did not answer but he finally said, "Okay, I won't."

"I'm by myself so much now. I could come over, you know, a lot." Then, "Or you could come to my house."

A moment passed. Just above a whisper she said, "I could make it real good for you."

The surge of his blood made Wendell slow to answer. "You mean, now?"

"Yes."

He heard her get up from the chair. Later he would think, as a very small point in defense of himself, that his delay before he turned around amounted to a surly nod toward a ghost of decency.

Wendell could remember in detail a good many tumbles in bed with women, including previous ones with Tricia, but not any that was much like this one. It was all done without a strictly human sound exchanged between them, starting with the moment when, in her bedroom in wraithy moonlight, in front of the open door, she stood with her clothes lying where they had fallen around her feet. The night was warm but the sight of her standing white and still in her nakedness made just for an instant a breach like a draft of bitter air across his lust. It was only an instant, and out of it his blood came raging back. That her body at first was cold in his hands was only the more incitement to his violence.

But she endured, then welcomed it. If there was pain, pain he meant to give with all his furious and prolonged thrusting, it did not get reflected in her cries. No longer groans but cries, that in the blinding moments of his crisis reached him like echoes strangely flung back from empty rooms of the house.

But the real strangeness came afterwards as he lay at the edge of sleep. The ghostly figures seated in chairs were difficult to see, were gossamer shapes in the moonlight. What impressed him with a vividness far, far greater was his sense of the rigid shame-struck postures in which they sat looking at him.

Judging from the angle of light he could not have slept very long. A small turn of his head showed him that Tricia's eyes were open and he lay thinking that if he wanted to he could reach and take one of those moon-flushed breasts in his hand. He saw her blink. It was like a palpable start whose minute vibrations he imagined feeling in the bed under him. But nothing followed and after a time, despite the shadow lingering from that dream, he did put a hand on her. She did not seem to notice.

"You want me to let you alone?"

She made a sound that meant No. But there was not any other response, even when he took his hand away. Grown hostile in her silence he finally said, "I better go."

"Please don't."

"Why?" But he knew why. To fill the interval he said, "You-know-who might come home."

"Not tonight." Then, "We can do it again. Just wait a little while."

A ray of the moon defined her open eyes. There was nothing to hear, not her breathing, not even creaks and tickings such as old houses made in the night. He said, "Why don't you go visit your family, get away from here for a while?"

"They're dead," she murmured.

"What about your sisters?"

"They wouldn't want me. They resent me."

"You could go somewhere, anyway," Wendell said and lay watching her open eyes, feeling hostile again.

"Do you want me to go away?"

Restraining his vexation he said, "I don't mean that. I meant, for your own good. Just for a while."

She seemed about to say something, and did not. When she spoke again her voice was even fainter. "If I could just stop imagining things . . . sounds. I'm always hearing her up there. Just awhile ago. I thought I heard that sound she made, falling. She was lying right with her head by the door. I can still see her."

After a moment, "She told me to go lie down."

Some question not yet fully shaped receded in Wendell's mind. The words *Go lie down* were coming slowly back to him in a voice different from Tricia's. It was Mother's voice. Trying to call up his anger again he said, "You've got to stop wallowing in it."

"I keep hearing her say that. She said she would fix her own supper."

"Look." For an interval Wendell could not think what to say next. Then, "Think about all those other times, all those years, when she treated you like trash. Think about those."

Nothing followed, not even a blink of her upward-gazing eyes. Until finally, "She was lying there on the floor. So little-looking. If I just hadn't seen her lying there."

"I was there too, remember: you weren't by yourself," he said, hearing his defensiveness. In defense of a thing that was not quite true, was it?

"I keep thinking if I went up there I'd still see her . . . lying there."

"You wouldn't see anything," he said almost harshly. "Or hear anything either." In the same voice he added, "You want to go up there and look? I'll go with you. Maybe that's what you need."

She shook her head.

"Come on." Wendell, rising onto his knees, took her arm more roughly than he intended. "Come on. Let's see if there's a ghost or something." He pulled at her arm.

"Please don't."

His anger receding, he slowly let go. "Then get it out of your head . . . all of it. Do you want to come back to my house?"

Indecision kept her still for a time. "Let's stay here. We can make love again."

Love, he thought. For a moment it was as if the word obscured her meaning. He stayed, and succeeded at last in rousing his torpid blood, and hers, making the cries from her open mouth return like echoes from the hollow rooms.

Sometime before daylight with the moon hanging above the horizon he left her asleep, and back in his own room sank heavily into his bed. Next, at the end of a space like a passage of minutes only, blinding pain of the sun in his eyes confused with memory what he afterwards knew had been a dream. But not yet. He saw himself, as real as any memory, get up from her bed and passing through the open door move like his own shadow along the hall to where the steps came down. Around the front door through the fanlights rays of the moon poured in. He was naked. Feeling their gaze from the living room, his body hot with shame, he passed through the moon's refulgence and up toward the salving darkness overhead. There was not any darkness. There was too much light for his eyes, making him squint, making him finally squeeze his eyes down tight against the pain. This was how he stood in front of her door with the knowledge that she was looking at him—just looking, with contempt maybe, but maybe not. Then he was not even sure that this was the same old woman and he wanted so much to know that he opened his eyes. This was the moment of his desperation. He found that he was not able to see at all.

XVI

Around sunset of that same day Wendell had a different kind of visitor. He arrived, insistent at the front door, like a thing begotten from this long day's succession of restless hours. There was the knock, repeated and repeated again, as in despite of Wendell's pretense of absence. This sense of being caught in deception was what compelled him at last to go to the door.

To discover him there was the kind of shock that might come with an image abruptly recalled from a harrowing nightmare. There was the jolt, and for a time uncertainty about the substance of the figure hugely facing him across the threshold. The figure was real, of course. Wendell's affliction—for this at first was how he suffered the presence confronting him—came partly from his notion that in some way accidental, through a lapse of his in the course of the day, he had summoned this man to his door. In any case Wendell stood there in the helplessness of one stripped of his defenses.

In fact, he later thought, the cause was his nervousness, the work of that dream that had shadowed him through the day. It never had let him be. He did not know why, he only knew that this was behind his obsessive vigils at his window. About noon he had seen Tricia. She came onto the back gallery and like a person on the way someplace descended the steps. Going where? The answer was, nowhere. On the walk she stopped and stood with the sun's glare in her white face. Then as on a new decision she went back into the house. He waited. He thought of her climbing the stairs, and instantly knew she would not do that. Putter in the kitchen, go into her bedroom? Not the living room, where, he imagined, in drifts of moted noonday light the spectral faces barely might be seen.

He was never hungry, though in the morning he had forced himself to eat something out of the refrigerator. With effects unpleasantly different from his previous experience he indulged himself in the last of the coke. Beyond the soaring early phase when his sense of mastery seemed to have no bounds, slips and faults began to appear. There were treacherous places where he put his feet and objects that somehow changed themselves without his will's consent. Here was the lighted room, a parlor once, and Farrow leaning toward him. "My boy," he said. Sure in himself Wendell would have extended a warm hand to him except that the light went out. Cold on the dark back porch Wendell peered to see through the shadow veiling his face. This was a moment of fear and he escaped it only by turning his eyes another way. More than once, many times. Back in this morning's dream again he stood in blinded desperation confronting the brightness through her open door.

He would leave this place, this country. He would do it quickly, when night came, using Rathbone's car. At one point he did go to the closet and take out his two battered suitcases. But this was all, he left them where they sat, telling himself that it was only night he waited for. When the knocking started the first of his thoughts was that Farrow stood at his door.

It was he, the nameless preacher, looking down at Wendell without even the barrier of the screen door that his great hand held open. Wendell was conscious of words from the man's mouth but it was some moments before they became clear.

"We met each other over there, next door." His free hand gestured. "Mrs. Harker's funeral."

The voice. Wendell remembered. The hand, enormous, came toward him. It was to be shaken.

The handshake, the feeling of his own hand threatened

in the mawlike grip, made a blur of the name he heard spoken. But the man knew Wendell's name, and called him by it. It was on his lips when, unbidden, he stepped across the threshold and passing Wendell by stopped for a look around him. The empty hall and the staircase, the doors to left and right. A searching look, as if to discover all hidden things in this house.

Their moving into the living room had to have been the preacher's doing. Certainly he was the first to sit down, in the armchair close to the hall door where for another minute or two he continued his scrutiny of the place. "Hubert Dowlin's house," he finally said. "Once it was. He was a good man." His eyes, yellow through flecks of brown, were turned on Wendell now. The hush in the room was as it had been in that front hall next door.

"Mrs. Harker too," he said. "She's with the Lord now. For all her goodness in this world." He sat erect, the chair diminished by the bulk of him. His tongue came out and traced and wet his lips. "I see you knowed her, though."

"A little." Maybe he was heard. They were the first words he had managed.

"I saw you looking at her there. Looking and looking." His pause was like a question unfolding, directed at Wendell by the yellow eyes.

What answer? Wendell groped in his mind and failed. Did the failure show? This was when he did for a diversion a thing he had not intended to do. The sofa was there and, turning, he sat down on it. The consolation that now he need not meet the preacher's eyes made him able to answer, "I was just thinking about her." When no reply came he added, "I'd met her a couple of times."

Again nothing, not for a minute that seemed to produce an unnatural kind of quiet. Wendell's glance discerned no change. The great black shoes were planted exactly side by side on the floor in front of the chair. Then,

"What were you thinking? I could see you thinking."

Wendell made the stillness this time, too long a stillness,

148

feeling the man's gaze intent on his parted lips. "I don't know. About being dead. The things you think."

"What things?"

"I don't know. Just that you're dead."

The man made some movement, Wendell heard it. The voice, more familiar than ever, said, "The body, just the body. And that will rise up. Miss Emma's will. To join her soul at the Throne."

Emma, then: that was her name. But he thought he had once known this. The reflection was dislodged by some brusque movement that struck the tail of his eye. It was the man's head, now thrust a little toward Wendell, the lips set to speak.

"Miss Tricia, you met her too?"

He had to unstick his tongue. "She invited me over. Neighborly. That's when I met her . . . Miss Emma."

Was the man waiting for more? His stillness seemed to demand it. Wendell's mouth came open and he heard himself say, blundering, "In the kitchen. We had tea. She . . . " He stopped it here, barely did. Fool. He had to set his teeth, feeling the eyes read him. But last sunrays in the room were abruptly extinguished.

"You ain't seen her anymore, since Miss Emma passed?"

But how could he mean anything? To say No by shaking his head seemed to Wendell the lesser risk. This was what he did, trying by glances afterwards to tell whether he was believed. Less visibly now the man's body stirred.

"It was the Lord sent me here, Wendell. His voice come to me. I been here before already but you was gone." He paused as if to let his words take hold. "But that never stopped His voice in my heart. His love's a thing don't never stop . . . till finally it's too late."

It was the old tent-meeting voice as vivid as yesterday.

"It's not any secret from His eyes, Wendell. And no dark thing that won't be brought to light. That's what He sent me to tell you. To open your heart and let His light come in. Before it's too late, boy."

Wendell could see him under the tent raging in the glare of the bleak light-bulbs. Stupid, bully: what could he know?

"God's merciful, though, enduring to all. No sin so vile that He ain't willing to pardon. I come here to go down on my knees with you." Already perched he put his hands on the chair arms. His tongue again, slowly tracing and wetting his lips in the glow of last daylight. "No matter your sins be black as hell. Repent, boy, repent your sins."

The words in Wendell's throat receded. He was a fool, bluffed by stupid fears. A surge of anger brought the words to his lips. "What sins? How do you know I've got any sins?"

Then it was as if he hung suspended there, with nothing real beneath the weight of this sofa where he sat. Poised in a chair of shadows now, the slow tongue going the round of his darkening lips, the man watched him. If this was the purest moment of hatred Wendell had ever felt, it was not enough: his effort to meet him eye-for-eye failed, and failed again. Or was this only because the dark was growing at such a rate.

"It's in your face, Wendell. Don't make it worse with lies."

It, the man had said *it*. "Make what worse? You're the liar. All you say is lies."

"I can see it. It's on your soul like a stain deep-dyed."

But he could see nothing. It was night in the room, blinding night, a curtain across his face. "Name it, then," Wendell said. "What is it?"

"It needs to be you to name it, Wendell. Save yourself."

"Yeah. Me. So you can find out . . . anything you can. When you don't know a goddamn thing."

"Blaspheming won't help you. The devil got no power against His name."

"Fishing. That's all you're doing. Bringing *her* in like you did. And that old woman. Just because I went over there a few times, just neighborly. Just because you saw me looking at her there. You think . . . "

Had something happened? *He* was the cause, though Wendell could not discern any movement or change in the

150

heaped-up bulk of darkness where the man sat. Then Wendell heard,

"Think what?"

"Think I, Tricia and me . . . " His voice ran out, draining away, submerged at last in some ultimate depth of stillness.

"You and Tricia . . . ?"

The breath that Wendell drew deep in his lungs made him able to speak again. "What about me and Tricia? If you know anything, say it."

"You say it."

"Liar."

"Get down on your knees, boy. Confess it."

Wendell was suddenly on his feet. "Get out!"

"She'll go along with you. I seen it in her. God give me eyes to see."

This was another perfect silence. Wendell groped for the sofa arm. "Where? When did you *see* her? You're lying again."

"Today. *He* sent me."

A trick, another trick. "Get out! Get out of here!" It was his echo, flung back late like a different voice from the empty hall upstairs, that told him he had shouted.

But something, maybe by his voice, had been made uncertain. Into the bulk of darkness where the man sat, in the tone almost of a question, Wendell said "Liar," and waited. No answer, nothing came back: gone? Straining against the dark he took a step and then another one. But this was the point at which he knew beyond uncertainty that the man was not only there but ready to speak again.

"Get out!" Wendell shouted, his last words as he turned and blundered his way to the staircase in the hall.

Although Wendell sat perched on the edge of his bed for some unmeasurable long time he had not heard the man leave. How not, in such a stillness? . . . unless he was still there. Finally urged by desperation Wendell stood in the dark hall outside his door. There was nothing to hear. The thought that some unaccountable lapse of his attention was to blame set him moving at last, despite that all his effort at stealth could not keep the floorboards silent.

There was a light switch at the head of the stairs but it was awhile before his hand located it and a longer while before he gathered the force to turn it on. In the explosion of light he stared with blind eyes down where the living-room door would be. It appeared in a blur, first framing the dark and then the chair, which was empty. The chair was empty. But fixing on this certainty did not at first diminish the rate at which his blood was pounding.

With still some caution he descended and paused in front of the empty chair. Then in sudden clarity he turned and almost at a run passed through the kitchen and out, through the hedge and the garden weeds and the path between the boxwoods. Prudence somehow stopped him there but only for a glance: the single car was Tricia's.

She was not in the lighted kitchen and the door was locked. He tapped at the glass, tapped again harder, and waited. Too long, he would try her window. In the same instant he saw her, or thought he did, a face afloat in shadow through the kitchen door to the hall. Was he mistaken? In a voice barely subdued he called her name. The shape of her in a dark bathrobe entered the light and came toward him.

Wendell had already spoken before she got the door quite open. She looked up at him, without an answer.

"Did that preacher come see you today?" he repeated.

Her lips parted but nothing more.

"Did he?"

"What preacher?"

"The big man. That was here that day, before the funeral. I don't know his name."

"Nobody came today."

"Yesterday? Any day?"

She blinked, a heavy drooping and lifting of her lids. "No. Reverend Sawyer, a few days ago."

That old man with snow-white hair. "Not him. A big man, real big. He was here that day. Didn't you see him?"

She shook her head. "Why?" she murmured.

A lie, then. Liar. But something was wrong. Was it she, the white face, the hair? He saw against the light how her hair, loose strands and wisps of it, obscured like a sort of disordered halo the silhouette of her head. "You don't even know him, at all?" That his voice had an unintended edge showed in her face.

"I would tell you. You know I would." Then, "Tell me what's the matter."

"He told me he came to see you. Like he meant you told him things. Today."

Tricia looked at him with eyes that seemed dark in her face. No, that preacher was the liar. Wendell said, "A trick, I think. He's got a notion somehow. To trick me. He's got no way to know." A moment followed in which his mind seemed locked in a vision of that empty chair.

"Who is he?"

Wendell heard this finally. "I don't know, not his name. I remember him from way back. At a tent meeting. He acted like . . . He kept trying to make me repent." The trick, maybe, was Wendell's own, played upon himself. "They do that, though, don't they? Try to scare you. To everybody. Don't they?"

Her wide eyes, darker than blue, seemed fixed on his open mouth.

"Don't they?"

"Yes."

"That's it, then, I'm a fool. He just picked me out of a hat. Grist for his mill. He didn't know anything." After his long breath of relief he began to wish he could see a change come in her face.

"I was a fool. Nobody knows anything. Just you and me." He put Farrow out of his mind.

"I think I remember him now," Tricia said.

"What?" Though he heard this it was too much like a thought whispered inside his head.

"I think he was the one that always used to send her a present at Christmas."

Her? Tricia meant the old woman. "Go on," he said.

"It was because she helped his family when he was little. They were poor."

He had to wait, longer this time, so long that he vaguely heard the sound of crickets in the yard behind him.

"I remember seeing him once or twice. I think his name's something like . . . Sears, maybe."

"Sears?"

"I don't know for sure, I can't remember." She was looking beyond him and he saw that a change had come, defining her eyes and pallid lips. It was because the full moon had crested the trees. She seemed to be looking at it. She said, "I remember they were nice presents . . . expensive." And finally, "He must have loved her." She went on looking at the moon, evidently, with her lips parted.

This continued for a time in which, as if her manner was the obscure cause of it, he could feel the slow return of his panic blood. Farrow came back to his mind. He said, "It's nothing to worry about, forget it. I have to go."

Her hand was suddenly on his arm. "Please don't. Come in for a while."

"I have to," putting her hand away.

"We could make love," she whispered.

"I'll try to come back," he said and left her.

XVII

When a police car came in sight on the street Wendell stepped behind a tree. Then he remembered: they were his cohorts, therefore friends. He hurried on and, passing up the alley where tonight no children played, he ducked through the shrubbery and saw the high-up light burning.

In moonlight filtered through foliage close to the porch the seated figure was visible. Wendell, approaching, did not know exactly what stopped him in mid-stride for a moment—some notion made unclear by the steady pulsebeat in his head. But he was seen, watched. He went on and at the foot of the steps he heard Farrow's voice. "Good you showed up. About to send for you."

On the porch Wendell opened his mouth to speak, but Farrow was ahead of him. Another one, Farrow was saying, bigger than the others. In a different place this time, though—down in Chambliss County. Then it was something about Wendell, about his job. "Going to make you my right hand, boy."

But a pause followed these words, a long pause in which Wendell endured the scrutiny of eyes that were obscurely visible to him now. "Set down there," Farrow said.

Wendell let go. "That preacher I told you about. He came to my house, awhile ago. It was like he was trying to worm it out of me. With tricks. He said he talked to Tricia. Like he had got it out of her. But he didn't, she said she hadn't seen him . . . That's what she said."

In a gauzy spill of moonlight that defined the round of his head Farrow waited.

"I'm sure she's telling the truth. It's just she's not taking it good. She's . . . I don't know. If he was to come and push her. I don't know."

There was no response, not a stir of movement. Then, "Set down there."

Wendell did, without consciousness of the act. "Named Sears, she thinks. He was friends with the old woman. Because . . . He'd have to be a mind reader. There's no way else he could know." Then, faintly, "Is there?"

Still no answer came.

"He kept saying 'it.' Like he knew what 'it' was, like he didn't mean just some ordinary bad thing. I don't think I slipped up. I don't think. It's just . . . There's something about him."

"What about him?" Farrow's voice barely parted the stillness. But Wendell heard him. The trouble was finding an answer. In a voice as doubtfully audible as Farrow's he said,

"I don't know."

Either Farrow had moved his head or else the spill of moonlight now reached him from a somewhat different angle. Though not in very much detail Wendell could see his face and see, just before Farrow spoke, darkness appear along the straight line where his lips met. "I checked on him already. She told you right. It's Sears."

Watching his mouth, Wendell again saw the darkness appear.

"Lives out there at Duncan's Ford. In a trailer. By hisself, no family or nothing."

That was noplace, Duncan's Ford, an abandoned store by a bridge.

"When he ain't off skinning the sheep . . . or nosing in other folks' business."

There was something different on the air—an ever-so-faint disturbance, as it were, engendered by these words. Still trying to get hold of it Wendell said, in a tone almost of conviction, "But he couldn't know anything. How could he?"

"How come he came to see you?"

156

Wendell hesitated. "An accident, probably. I caught his eye someway. Another lost soul. That's the way they do."

"Yeah. They do. But I ain't a man likes a coincidence. This here's a big one."

A sort of clotting like the sudden effects of a cold coming on gathered in Wendell's throat. He had to clear it before he could say, "He couldn't ever prove anything. He doesn't *know* anything."

"Maybe not."

A moment passed. "It was probably me, taking him wrong, because I was scared. He probably just meant to save my sinful soul . . . like they always do." Wendell hung suspended in his own hush.

"Maybe so."

This was Farrow's only response until, after a moment, he distinctly moved his head. The result was another change of light on his face and in that instant an effect that Wendell's own disordered imagination must have distilled for him. If the moment was *like* that of his first encounter with Farrow, it was only as a nightmare might resemble a merely uncanny dream. This time he *saw* the face: toadlike on a neckless head up-rounded from rounded shoulders. No lips to the long straight mouth that looked as if a razor had made it, and eyes without any lids. The bulging eyes were what he remembered best, with jewellike points of moonlight where pupils ought to be.

This was how it seemed for the short or long time before another movement of Farrow's head put an end to it. The face was veiled again, if not its image in Wendell's mind. The low voice, unchanged, was saying, "You be down at Bison Springs tomorrow, six o'clock in the evening. Stand around the feed store there, fellow named Bruno'll find you. Putting you in charge this time. They'll do just what you tell them."

No difference in the voice, the accustomed voice. Suddenly the thought was a comfort, casting doubt on the vision stuck in Wendell's mind.

"You got it straight?"

157

"Named Bruno," he said, like a name he had to unearth.

"He'll find you, no problem." Then, "Bringing you on, boy. I got plans for you."

Plans. It was like a strange word hovering in front of his mind's eye. Then the preacher took its place, and all at once Wendell was conscious that in the stillness enclosing them he could hear nothing, not even cricket sounds. The question taking shape in his thoughts never got farther than that. Or did it, in a way that escaped his hearing? The words that Farrow chose this moment to speak were too much like an answer. "I'll do the worrying, you just tend to your job. So go on now and get your rest."

Rising from his chair Wendell heard him speak again. "Just keep on being sweet to little Tricia. She'll get all right by and by." And from the steps, arrested yet again by Farrow's voice, he heard, "She's there by herself tonight too, ain't she?"

"What happened? Please tell me."

This, Wendell thought, was the third time she had spoken to him in this way, in a whisper, with the difference now that she was holding his hand against her naked breast. And looking, gazing at him, his face exposed in rays of the moon from her window. He said, "It's nothing to worry about. Not really. It's just me."

"Please. It's me, too." She kept his hand there, enclosed in her warm flesh. "It's about the preacher, isn't it?"

Wendell could see the bridge and, where it mounted to span the creek, that rotten hulk of a store. In the parklike space behind it was where the trailer would be. Nothing else, no traffic much, not a soul for a mile. In moonlight. In filtered moonlight on the porch he was seeing Farrow's face. But that was an illusion.

"Please."

"You said you'd seen him? Really seen him? The preacher."

"Yes. A couple of times, I think."

"It's like I dreamed him. But I couldn't have."

Her hand tightened on his. "Does he know? Tell me."

"I can't. I don't know. I really don't."

A time passed and the moonrays no longer touched their bodies. Though she held his hand less tensely she had not let go. He felt the heave of breath she finally drew. "Are they going to find out?"

It was in his mind to say No but his tongue was not willing. "Are they?"

Wendell heard this clearly enough but what she said next, after some moments, at first escaped his understanding. It came to him with a shock: "I wish they would find out."

"No you don't." Now it was his hand gripping hers, with force enough to make her flinch a little. He had turned toward her. "Think about it. For God's sake. Think what would happen." She was looking at the ceiling. He let go of her hand. "Think about prison. And the trial, and everybody knowing. And Joe, think about him."

There was light enough that he could see how her eyes were wide open. "Don't talk crazy," he said, feeling his mouth get running on its own. "I'm in it too, I put you to it, because I had to. Because . . ." Prudence for the space of a second stopped his rattling tongue. "It's just because we're scared, scaring ourselves . . . it'll go away. Just wait awhile, both of us. You'll see. Think about the way she did you, all those years. And the things we talked about. Like being free from crap. It just takes awhile, to stop scaring ourselves, that's all. If we just . . ." His hesitation prolonged itself, grew into a hush. It became a hush in which he seemed to hear, as from someplace the other side of silence, his faint voice gibbering on.

He heard a real voice, hers. "Why did you?"

"What?" he finally murmured.

"Why did you put me to it?"

His mouth came open, but where was a lie that would answer? He made no answer, and what she said next, long afterwards, had nothing to do with the question. He saw her lips stir and then it came.

"You don't love me at all, do you? Even a little."

Looking back on that moment Wendell believed that he had come close to saying, "Yes, I do." This was what instinct first suggested, with the thought that such words were what she most needed now. For prudence' sake, for policy, to guard her and guard himself against what her remorse might bring. He even thought of better words, a little more plausible: "I didn't at first, but now . . ." He would take her hand. But somehow he did nothing, a nothing that made her finally say, "You don't have to answer. It would only be a lie."

Yet after a space he did do something, a thing that came on him by surprise. It was not design, it was impulse that moved him to reach and take her hand and hold it and keep on holding it for many minutes. In Wendell's memory these were vivid minutes, still returning to him the sense he had of a small warm imperiled resting place between the onslaughts of fear and anxiety. And he remembered wishing, what he never before had wished, for a sign that she too felt as he was feeling. But no sign came, no answer in the hand he kept on holding. Still he persisted on and on, dimly aware at last of a bird singing out there in the yard.

It was after the bird stopped that she spoke again.

"I think it was me, all along. I was selfish. And mean."

"What?" he murmured.

"She didn't hate me. I just thought she did. Because I hated her. It was my fault she got angry like she did, and said things. I was such a little . . . nothing. I keep thinking about it, all the good things she did. For lots of people."

"That's not what you told me. All the time." There was a pressure against his heart.

"Oh I was such a nasty little fool."

Wendell let go of her hand. Rising onto his elbow he said, "That's just *now*, the way you're feeling now, looking back. Because you feel guilty. It's not true, you know it's not. That's what guilt does, distorts everything." His rattling tongue again.

But he could not leave her this way. "You've got to hang on, you'll ruin us both." Then, "Look, I'm not going away. I might have to go off sometimes but I'll be back. I promise."

This was a lie, though. The thought came suddenly, envisioning a plan settled since yesterday in his mind. On the floor by his closet the two suitcases stood. And Rathbone's car waiting. Atlanta first and then a plane somewhere, anywhere. He would go. He settled back onto his pillow, and waited.

"Why did you want me to do it?"

He considered answering. He did not, except to murmur, "I'll tell you sometime." Silence was best, he thought, prudent not only in his behalf but in hers as well. He took her hand back and limp though it was held it until he could see that her eyes had closed. He did not think she was really asleep but this was excuse enough. He got up quietly and dressed and with a whispered Goodnight that brought no response left the house. By the time he got back to his own room upstairs Wendell's thoughts had turned another way.

The trailer in the silent grove by the bridge: What if he went and warned him? But this was a question that would not stay for an answer. Instead, like a blow that scattered thought, the vision of Farrow's moonlit face appeared. When finally Wendell got up from his bed in the dark, his foot struck one of the suitcases.

Some frenzied minutes followed. One suitcase stuffed with his clothes lay on the bed, with only the straps yet to be buckled. He was tugging at these when the energy began to drain from his movements. Fool. He stood up straight, kept standing. He began to pace, telling himself that whatever might happen would not be the work of his hands. But, as he later wished to believe, it was not this thought only that brought him to such measure of resolution as he reached in that hour. Anyway he did not return to his packing.

Wendell did not have too much longer in which to go on thinking about the question. At a point where his thoughts had begun to run more slowly there came a new distress, from the telephone downstairs. Maybe he was late to hear it: when he arrived the receiver hummed in his ear. After this he hovered about within steps of the phone on the table.

This was how a slow time passed. But finally there was

something to catch his attention. By accident, though it must have been visible all this while, a glance toward the window picked up filigrees of light in the hedge between him and Tricia's house. That would be her kitchen window, but what about it? She in her kitchen late at night, maybe for something to make her sleep. But after many minutes, and on and on, the light kept burning. There was something at his heart.

He went out and stood with his face in the hedge, peering. Finding a place less dense, worming through, he gazed for a while at the high window before he quietly mounted the gallery steps. The kitchen was empty. He tapped on the glass, and later tapped again. The door was not locked. Standing on the threshold he called her name. All he could hear was the ticking of the big clock in the dining room.

The door to her room was shut and when after a faint knock or two he opened it she was obscurely visible on the bed, clothed in something now. "Tricia," he whispered. That thing at his heart took hold and, entering, he stood looking down at her. "Tricia." He could hear her breath, troubled breath, and he put a hand on her shoulder. Then he was shaking her, calling her name, hearing through the surge of his panic his own voice louder each time. Had her eyes opened? He thought they looked up at him for a second, and closed. After that for all his shaking and calling her name they would not open again.

There was an interval in which the things Wendell did and thought had to be untangled in his memory of them. Standing under the hall light tearing at pages of the telephone book, he could not keep fixed in his mind what he was looking for. A doctor, an ambulance. The tick of the clock kept twining in, tumbling among his thoughts. Sleeping tablets from the bottle empty on her table. On a page now a doctor's name had caught and fastened his eyes. Fastened, but this was all: the clock kept ticking. At length, no longer holding the book, he put his hand on the telephone. Then in a flash of clarity it was as if the word No spoke itself inside his head. For what would he be doing in this house?

Too late anyway: go home, put out the lights. This purpose, he would recall, was so clear in his mind that he made a small interior movement whose result should have been his setting out to enact it. The ticking clock, distinct drop after drop of sound falling into his consciousness, appeared to be the reason he did not. Or the *first* reason, because, as came slowly upon him, there was another sound requiring a greater intentness to discern. He thought it was a whispering somewhere, a secret voice or voices in the house. Then he thought it was Tricia, trying without strength to speak to him.

This was what Wendell imagined, hearing the voice grow clearer and words he was beginning to understand. Until he realized that this was his memory speaking, repeating a thing she had said mere hours ago. "You don't love me at all, do you? Even a little." His answer had been silence.

Of all the moments Wendell would remember, these in Tricia's hall that night had no rival ever for the stark pain they inflicted. Her words and then the silence deepening around him. In a curious brainsick way he stood listening, hopeful that he would yet hear his own voice, grown tender, return some decent answer to her question. There was not any answer. He could see himself there, with bleak light on his face, his jaw gone slack, the tips of keen white teeth exposed by the sagging underlip. Imagined or not, this was the face that portrayed him to himself in those stark moments.

Wendell did not think that this interval lasted more than a minute or two. He knew he came out of it with the suddenness of a purpose already decided on and that, as far as it went, he did what he ought to have done. Only withholding his name he made the call—to a woman who answered the phone. After that, in spite of the warning voice getting louder in his head, he did the things he was most glad he had done. He tried again to wake her. He lifted her up and with her head lolling against his cheek and shoulder he shook her and called her name and opened her white eyes. With a cloth from the bathroom he sopped her face and neck. No difference, though, except her breath that came with a strangling sound.

An idea that occurred to him came too late. With the thought to make her vomit he went and snatched open one kitchen cabinet after another, and found a jar of mustard. The sound of a car became audible. Though it went on past, it left him holding the jar in a stiffened hand. There might be time enough yet, he turned back toward her room. But the sound he heard now was a siren and he barely made it through the hedge before the headlights could catch him.

XVIII

A little after six in the evening Wendell followed the man, Bruno, out of Bison Springs south about nine miles where they turned off on a gravel road that climbed and descended through pine woods. A few minutes of this, passing two or three small farms, and then another turnoff. This road that was half washed out in places brought them down in twilight into a long creek bottom. One truck was there and a few men lounging about. Soon another truck appeared, bringing enough men to make up a full dozen. Bruno, fast-talking and suave in a fedora, stayed just long enough to give a few instructions, which included putting Wendell in charge.

This one was no longer much of an airstrip. Clumps of pine grew rank out of the crumbled pavement and where a hangar had once stood was nothing but a few collapsed and rusted girders. They worked in light from Coleman lanterns and sometimes headlights of the trucks. They cut the trees at pavement level, though letting them lie for now as camouflage, and hauled red clay and gravel from a bank near the edge of the woods. Except for one man Wendell had met in a motel room, named or thought to be named Larson, the men were strangers to him. Some of them knew each other and talked among themselves in accents he could identify only as northern. They did Wendell's bidding, though, quickly and exactly as directed.

It was hard work and every hour or so they took a break. Especially on toward the end of the night with the men sitting half-sprawled on a truckbed or the pavement, an interval of perfect stillness would sometimes fall. Or stillness broken only now and then by the cry of a nightbird or a distant bobcat's scream. Wendell's remedy at these times was to fetch up some remark designed to start the talk again.

But on a couple of occasions, there were intervals worse than these when, at some rumor of alarm, not only the voices but every light went out almost as one. Not a whisper then, and men like frozen shadow-shapes in the gloam of the waning moon. These were Wendell's moments of no defense. Tomorrow night, he would try to think, clutching once more at the notion that he would be gone. It was not any use, nothing to pit against the anguish coiled around his heart. This was the first night but the two that followed were in no way different.

But compared to his days the nights were interludes of peace and clarity in which he moved from one intelligible objective to another. His drive home in first daylight was a progress back into a state of mind that not infrequently approached real dementia, when his anguish produced a flat and obstinate denial that seemed to put him in a world of his own making. It simply had not happened, none of it had happened. Even that first morning's inescapable memory of parked cars and silent bustle around the house next door lost its substance in this world. His answer to this and to every threatening thought was like an act of deliberate blindness, or like living where doors had, no matter the cost, to remain tight shut. To keep them this way was the chief business of his daylight hours, and his chief support, proclaimed by the suitcases standing next to his bed, was his dream of imminent escape. It later struck him as surely a little demented that he had contrived for nearly three days to keep himself as secure in this dream as if it really was a resolution.

Of course there were times when illusion failed him. In his sleep there was no defense and even the shock of bright daylight was slow to expel the dreams from his mind's eye. There was Tricia haggard like a ghost, failing into darkness. The trailer in the grove by the bridge, Farrow's nightmare face. There was also, to conclude the afternoon of the second day, a face that did not come to him in his sleep.

166

It appeared to him in a rush of confusion as he pulled the front door open. For all the determined evasiveness of his thoughts a knock at his door was like a thing he had been expecting and poised upright on his bed he had told himself, Here it comes. But the face, the bloated figure with badge and pistol confronting him from the porch belonged to Chief Dutch Doolin.

A friend, Wendell thought, watching the fat pink lips fold and unfold themselves around the words they were speaking. "Had to be *somebody* phoned the doctor. Wasn't nobody else that lives around here. They set me to find out."

The lips had shut like a purse, he was waiting. A denial came first to Wendell's mind but he stopped it there. If he said Yes . . . ? Why had he not thought about this? Doolin was watching intently.

"Eve'body thinks it just about had to be you," Doolin said, and paused. "I reckon what happened was, you noticed something, lights on late and all. Her by herself. Got uneasy and went over there. That about right?"

What must have been there already, the irony in his face, was all of a sudden obvious to Wendell.

"Door unlocked. You tried to help her, made that call and ev'ything. How come you run off, though? That's what's funny."

The eyes were bright and close together, tucked like a hog's eyes over the spreading jowls. He needed only the big male's tusks.

"I expect you just got to thinking, though, about being over there at night where you didn't have no natural bidness to be. Look funny. And you a little scared too, you a young man and somebody dying on you. I figure probably you heard that siren coming and just lit out. Ain't that right? I'll tell him that if you want me to."

It was the unmistakable leer of secret fellowship that brought the revulsion up into Wendell's throat. Farrow had primed him. In that moment, that expectant leer, Wendell could not manage even to nod his head.

"That the way you want it? I got it right, ain't I?"

No! Liar! He could all but hear himself hurling the words into Doolin's hog face. What he finally answered out loud was only a muted "That'll do."

That would do, would *have* to, Wendell thought, seeing in afterimage the fat pink lips give shape to his lies for him. His long moment there in the wake of Doolin's departure was an experience of degradation that gave him his final meaning for the word. He had it still for company in his room, pictured still in Doolin's lips and bloated colluding face. He would leave now, tonight. Half an hour later he did leave, but only to make the turn that put him once more on his route to the airstrip.

Again there was a measure of peace out there under the stars and the late-rising moon, and maybe if there had been no sequel to the afternoon's event Wendell would have been able to keep on as before. But there was the fated sequel, waiting for him late next day at the end of a spell of sleep.

Finding he needed food for a change and nothing on hand he started out to walk uptown. There was hedge to screen his passing in front of Tricia's house and he had no warning when, just steps ahead, a figure appeared through the gap where the walkway entered. He was looking at Joe.

Wendell had seen him before from a distance only, a tall round-shouldered man who walked with his head bent a little forward, as in humility. Now he had his head up, surprised maybe by what he saw in the face looking back at him. A car went by.

"You're Wendell Corbin, aren't you?"

Wendell could nod.

"I was just coming over to see you, to thank you. I know you tried to help her." His deep-set eyes with bluish crescents under them had a cloudy look. "I wanted to thank you." A visible contraction in his throat kept him still for a second. "Chief Doolin told me. I can understand why you didn't want to be over there when they came."

A lie? This thought that Joe did not believe it blazed in Wendell's mind for a second. How could he believe it?

"You did all you could. They found . . ." He diverted his eyes.

Found what? Then Wendell knew: the wet cloth, the mustard jar he had left somewhere. The man was not lying, not with such an expression. It was time for Wendell to say something but even as he cast about for words he saw that he was being spoken to.

"I'd take it kindly if you would."

He meant the house, for Wendell to come in, pressing it on him now. Wendell said No and No again but he went, in the foolish fear that his refusal might somehow be read. Up the walk, the porch steps, into the muted light astir with motes. Past the stairs and the living room he followed Joe in silence to the back of the hall, past the bedroom, into the kitchen.

"She stayed a lot in here. Read there at the table." He indicated a chair. He meant it for Wendell. "I'll get us coffee. A drink, if you want."

Wendell said No to this last and from the chair watched Joe about the business of getting coffee—a clumsy man who missed at pouring and made a spill on the counter. A clean kitchen otherwise, no mustard jar in sight. He heard the clock ticking.

"I sent Little Joe back this morning. And my cousin gone too. It's just . . . I don't know what to do with myself." He looked as if he was weighing the danger of picking up the cups. "I threw the rest of the flowers away. I hated the flowers." With minutest care he lifted the cups and, bringing them to the table, put down the dripping one at his own place. Seating himself, "I don't know where things are," he said.

Wendell concluded his nod with his eyes fixed on his own cup. Joe was watching him, preparing something. It was:

"You all were friends, weren't you . . . kind of?"

Wendell's throat came unstuck. "Yes. A little. She asked me over a couple of times, to talk. About books."

Joe's fingers, with bitten nails, closed and unclosed on his cup. "She liked to read books. Deep books I couldn't make a thing out of. She said you knew all about books. She said you were a writer."

A writer. He thought about his writing. Still there in his table drawer. He gave a nod deliberately obscure. Out on the gallery birds were twittering and now he thought it was maybe this that had shifted his attention. It was not. He saw Joe's eyes. They might have been staring at some desolate and inexplicable revelation.

"I keep thinking," Joe said. "It must have been me, part of it. Because I was too dumb. And couldn't understand her. And she was lonesome. Even when I was at home." He paused as if for a still harder look. "I was always off on trips, leaving her by herself. And Mama gone too. And Little Joe. In this big old empty house. What am I going to do with this old empty house?" Now it might have been the sound of emptiness he was listening to. There was gray in the hair that looked all black from a distance.

"It always was like Mama's house. But I thought, after she died, Tricia and me . . ." He did not finish. He gazed past Wendell, at the door to the dining room maybe, where the clock ticked.

Wendell finally murmured, "You've still got your son," and instantly, painfully wished he had not spoken.

"He won't want to come back here. It's nothing to come back to. I'm going to shut this house up and leave tomorrow."

Was there anything Wendell could say, dared to say? Even *I'm sorry* would be a sort of lie. He would leave now. But how could he leave in silence? He listened to the clock.

Then Joe's voice, changed, forced out of his throat, "Why do you think she did it?"

Wendell could feel on his lowered face the desperate weight of the man's stare. He did what he could not help but do, shake his head at the mystery.

"Didn't she ever say anything . . . when she talked to you?"

Another lying shake of Wendell's head. In returning silence a thought bloomed so vividly in his mind that it seemed the actual words "It was me, I did it" had tumbled out of his mouth. He even glanced and saw in a spurt of panic what seemed like confirmation: the hanging lip and glazed look of a man stunned by a blow. A few seconds, it was not true. Joe said, "She wouldn't have talked about it," and sent his tortured gaze beyond Wendell again. Wendell's hand was trembling and he hid it in his lap.

Wendell thought that his moment of panic in the kitchen was what had made him able to take his leave with a certain grace. For where truth was not even a choice, why scruple about a lie? So at the front door, where Joe with his glazed face thanked him again, Wendell said the expected, the necessary things. Because they were necessary, because there was no way to undo the things already done.

This was a reflection that afterwards brought him an interval of doubtful solace. He ate the food he did not taste and back in his room in the presence of the packed suitcases on the floor he thought of the distance already growing between those things and him. He thought of Cayman Island and how in that white light the starkest of his memories was less than real. Receding things, falling into the past. The old thought flared in his mind: Why not now? He had his money, even a passport! But his flush of excitement was gone in a minute or two.

Wendell was later confident, and was all but confident at the time, that he could have managed it all right, without much real danger. Quick to Atlanta and out by plane. Or even something a good deal less dramatic. If his gut-fear of Farrow was a reason, it was not reason enough. Why had he not done it, then, who had long since committed himself to the notion that the good was only what was good for him? The answer, or the part of it that did not remain a mystery, was also the explanation for his unexpected decision that night at the airstrip. If it was to be called an actual decision. In fact it was like a thing given or thrust upon him suddenly in consequence of what had preceded the night.

Well up in the afternoon, in the wake of those high moments when his dream of escape was on him, Wendell had tried to go to sleep. It seemed in reach, he felt himself sinking toward it. What followed instead and continued on were most like seizures that afterwards put him in mind of highs gone bad, when vision after relentless vision afflicted the inner eye. Haggard Tricia kept coming back, looming out of the dark, and Mother that day he had blundered into her kitchen. Farrow, the same each time, like a nightmare in moonlight on his porch. And Sears, the preacher, though Wendell never was able to see him clearly. What he could see clearly under the moon was the trailer there by the bridge at Duncan's Ford. An empty trailer . . . too late. But this last was a thought intruding, producing itself each time as the image faded. That night at the airstrip in their final break before dawn, this thought raised to life again was the force that spurred him to act.

He sat, in a quiet stirred only by chirping crickets, on the pavement next to one of the trucks. A man called Skeet sat darkly above him on the truckbed, blotting out the moon, never speaking. When the stillness began to prey on Wendell he opened his mouth to say something. There was no need. On the other side of the truck a bass voice he recognized as Zimmer's was speaking. Wendell missed the first words and the first reply of a second voice but then he heard Zimmer say,

"Had my suspicions about him all along, worked with him a couple of times. The guys up-top had their eyes on him, though. They don't miss much. Got narc-busters you don't know who they are. Pros, though. Real bad guys."

"That was him they found in the swamp, wasn't it? Venutti?"

"Yeah. Brains blown out. That's mostly the way they do it. Right up under the back of your skull. Bingo and that guy's dog meat. Tough, but that's what they sign up for."

The stillness shut down and after a space the whisper of crickets came back. Too late. The thought stood in Wendell's mind. Moments later it had the shape of a question and after that by a decision he could not remember making he was on his feet and telling the men it was time get back to work. From that moment until he saw first daystreak in the east he was straining against himself, barely in possession. Was it too late? He had the feeling, though mainly afterwards, that he blundered in the excuse he gave for his abrupt departure. Out on the road, driving fast, he could recall nothing of the words he had used.

At sunrise that clouds obscured, where the highway curved and a gas station marked the place, he turned onto a gravel road that ran between solid woods. He was sure he had not mistaken the way, yet uncertainty took hold of him. Driving slower and slower, passing a crossroads finally, he coasted to a stop. This could have been his undoing. The question while he sat there with the engine idling was what exactly he had said to explain his sudden departure. Go back? Go home? Some easy lie would mend it. When he put the car in motion again he thought his intention was to go home. Except that in almost the next moment his eyes discovered up ahead the steel bridge over the creek, he might have done so. Instead he crossed the bridge and saw under trees beyond the store the trailer in the gray of morning light.

There was a car beside the trailer. He saw this in the instant he stopped: it was not too late. But the sight was one that also kept him sitting awhile in his own car and, once out, reluctant to let go of the door. A sudden breeze tingled across the back of his neck. Maybe he was seen, watched. He let go. Descending the bank he crossed the ditch and, walking straight into the imagined gaze upon him, did not stop until he faced the high door in the side of the trailer.

Nothing happened. A bird, a heron, screeched from somewhere along the creek. He took a step forward and lifted a hand that for a second stood poised there in front of his face. He softly knocked. Nothing happened.

He knocked, louder this time, and stood tensely listening

for many seconds before it came to him: the man was not here. His instant feeling of reprieve lasted only until he turned his head and saw the car parked by the tree.

There was the man's car. Wendell kept hearing, like a sound out of another dimension, repeated cries of the heron on the creek. The thought Go home entered and passed out his mind.

It might have been a long time before he turned back and lifted his hand and closed it on the doorknob. The door came open. In time he recognized that the sound of flies buzzing inside the trailer was his imagination only. He put a foot on the high step.

There was nobody in the trailer. This was a fact slow to come clear, shaping itself in the aftermath of what his first stunned glance had seemed to show him. It was a cot from which the spill of covers over the edge mocked the form of a man with his head to the floor. For a time while his gaze scanned about him as if for the hidden body among the clutter, the question Where? hung like a bat in his mind. A Bible lying open on a scarred desk stopped his eyes for a second, before they moved on and came to rest on the table beside him. There was a plate with food from a meal half-eaten. What this might mean came slowly but he got it straight at last. Interrupted? And the door, why hadn't the man locked the door when he left?

That Wendell had sat down in this only chair at the table came to him as a sort of remote surprise. It was like waking up with his gaze locked into a vision of half-eaten food on a plate. This was where the man was sitting when they came. The fork that lay across the rim of the plate was just as he had put it down when he heard them at his door. Had it happened then, or later? In a swamp somewhere, like Venutti, the great bulk of him floating in his grave. Another one, then, to go with the two that had been Wendell's score until now? A question? But where was the reason permitting him to put this as a question?

Wendell did not know how long he sat there but he remembered how the interval reached its peak in one extended and stricken moment of astonishment. It was real, he had done these things—he the Wendell seated here in the chair of another one, the third, whose death he had caused. He knew why in such a moment the thought of his unfinished book came back. Because the Wendell in that book had come to life in the end.

A car passing out on the road brought him to his feet. In the quiet that followed he heard above the sound of his heart another sound. It was the heron's cry. Then he was on the ground at the foot of the steps and hearing the cry again as he moved in a sort of stony fascination across the clearing and into the trees along the creek bank. There from a log at the water's edge the heron took flight and noisily vanished among the trees.

There was a pool, with water as still as a pond and silver under the clouds. Maybe here. The sheen on the water's face gave back nothing except the sky. Maybe here, deep down, weighted against the bottom. Hearing the sound of another car he stiffened. Again the sound diminished and failed and afterwards, immersed in his own blind stare at the water's surface, he experienced a change like a shift of light inside his head. This was his private swimming hole where he, a boy, stood on the bank for a dive. With drawn breath, from a world of hateful voices, he would plunge to the bottom and, finding a root, hold himself there in the silvery drift of silence. Then up for breath and down, back into his silvery dream.

Something interrupted—or was it only imagined? It was in his mind that the passing car he had heard did not after all keep going. He moved a few steps and, sheltered by a tree-trunk, surveyed the clearing and the road beyond. His car was up there, nothing else. But the road both ways from his car was hidden.

Wendell's long vigil beside the tree was not interrupted. But when he came out into the open he was walking fast in a straight line toward his car.

XIX

In later days Wendell came to hold an abstract opinion he would have described this way:

We know very little about objective reality and the part of it we do perceive is not only a mere fraction of the whole but a fraction interpreted or pictured according to the structure of our mental faculties. Time and space belong to us and not to *that* reality: the appearance otherwise is an imposition of our own. Because as a species we share the same kind of faculties, we all see what we do see in much the same way. So we accept as real and call "rational" the perceptions common to us. This certainly makes sense: for the sake of order and coherence we have to accept it. Even so, might not this view of reality be a kind of mistake? Suppose a mind for some reason operating without the category of time. Can we say that its perceptions, because they differ from most, are necessarily invalid? Shouldn't we say instead that such a mind may be the one privileged to see things hidden from others?

This was an opinion that gave support to beliefs Wendell continued to hold about some of his experiences that summer, especially in the final days. The commonsense explanation was of course hysteria, brought on by fear and remorse intensified by physical exhaustion—the stuff of hallucination. But such an explanation never satisfied him. Events, or seeming events, of the day and night that followed his visit to the preacher's trailer were among the instances he remembered.

It was afternoon before he got back to his room. From the trailer, with eyes fastened straight ahead on the road, he drove to Bison Springs. He found a public telephone and, nervously on display in the glass booth, blundered his way through at last to an agent whose name remained unclear. So, to the agent, was Wendell's name until he twice repeated it. This was the hardest thing. The moment when the voice recited it clearly back to him was one in which Wendell's tongue seemed to have gone dead in his mouth. Sometime later with the receiver humming in his ear Wendell found himself in vague possession of the fact that he was to be part of a trap.

At least up to a point the voice on the phone made a difference. That at dusk, on his usual way to the airstrip, he was to meet this man for instructions was not, however, the heart of it. For a person confined a long time in darkness even the briefest glimpse of a world out there in daylight is reassurance. It was this way in those minutes on the phone: for that brief space he was admitted once again to a condition of things clearly defined and certain in themselves. This was what gave him the boldness, after some hours of aimless delay, to go back to his room in Turnbull.

The result was one of those instances for which Wendell would not accept a sensible explanation. In a state of near-exhaustion he drove home trying to keep his mind fixed on the bottomless sleep that waited for him in his bed. Except his mind would not stay fixed. And once he had made the turn and stopped in the driveway the fear that had been threatening all along took him by the throat. He knew as a fact that hidden among the foilage in the vacant lot beside him eyes were watching. Approaching the back door in the aftershock of that fear he experienced a sense of bodily detachment, as if the accustomed weight of Earth had all of a sudden diminished under his feet. So fear and exhaustion might just as well have been the cause of what he experienced with such conviction a little afterwards.

The light in his room was gray and the black intervals in which he sometimes lay suspended were not really sleep. They were more like ominous and measureless prefaces, and

177

it was from one of these that he emerged already knowing what sort of thing his tight-shut eyes would see if he dared open them. The chill of the grave was supposed to come with ghosts, and it did, though maybe only in that the fear was enough to stop his pulse. He lay for so long in its presence that a bubble of clarity began to form in his mind. Shaping itself there was the word *hallucination* and on the strength of this he at last forced his eyelids open. What he saw was doubtful, without any certain outline, shadow failing into cloudy light. Much less doubtful, in a sort of icy aftermath, was a sound like whispering faintly breathed into the hollow of his ear. There were no words he could understand but there was terror—terror like a scream wedged tight in his throat. This happened not once but two times before he quit his bed.

Through an interlude between sleeping and waking, when thoughts at random flickered and went out in his head, he sat erect with his back to the living-room wall. What he seemed to know without thinking was that an uncertain but surely fearful issue stood somewhere in the offing. This was why his gaze kept running to windows across the room, where clusters of leaves on the shrubs outside took unexpected shapes. A face once, and once a hand. Because it would come, because his act of betrayal was known already.

But in time reason came back. A full hour before dusk Wendell stood at the kitchen door looking out. The yard and the ruined garden, detailed in the level gray of afternoon, hid no threat to him. It would have to come at night, would it not? And how could they know? Yet the thought that he was safe for now was a comfort as frail as smoke. Lest those other thoughts overtake him he hurried out to the car.

He drove to the Grill, a natural thing. Forcing himself he ate something, feeling it like a lump in his shrunken belly. There was nobody on the street outside and he drove out of town with never a glimpse of any car behind him.

The turnoff and then another mile brought him to the end of a long curve and a field of sedge brush. At the far edge of the field in last clear daylight he saw the decrepit barn and, beside it, a green car parked. A man stood leaning against the car, watching as Wendell turned and came to a stop among the weeds. A lean man. His bald head reflected the steely skylight. Stepping forward, he said,

"Corbin?"

Wendell nodded. It was done.

The man showed him a badge. "Earl McCabe," he said. Hands on the sill, propped on sinewy arms, he observed Wendell's face through the window while he talked. "You do just what I say, you'll get a deal," he said. "Probably get clear off. Okay?"

Clear off? It was not that Wendell failed to understand him.

"Go free, I mean. You help us and we help you. Okay?"

Wendell thought he said Yes. He listened, compelling his mind to listen. A trap to catch them, set for the night when the plane would land. "When's that going to be?" McCabe asked. Four, maybe five days, Wendell was not sure. Where? Wendell could answer this one. McCabe wrote in a little book, his bald head bent to see in the failing light. Then it was names he wanted, only the big ones for now. "You ought to know one or two, don't you?"

Finally Wendell said, "Just one."

"Okay." McCabe held his pen ready. After a time he said, "Okay, what is it?" observing Wendell. "You need to hurry, don't you?"

"Jason Farrow." It was out of his mouth, audible, after a second written in ink on a page of McCabe's little book.

McCabe was looking at him again. "You know anything about him? Where he lives?"

"In Turnbull," Wendell murmured.

McCabe's pen touched the page, then stopped. "You mean *that* Farrow? Owns the car agency?"

Wendell met the brightening eyes.

"You sure?"

"Yes."

Giving a little whistle McCabe wrote it down. "You *damn* sure?"

"I'm sure."

"Okay," McCabe said. "Any others?"

Wendell gave him Halloway's name, if that was his name, describing the man, remembering the tiepin.

"Here." The piece of paper he handed Wendell had a phone number. "Call me early tomorrow. Do exactly like always. You'd better, you know. You know that, don't you?"

Wendell looked at him. "I think they killed that preacher."

"We're checking on it. Get going."

Because it was almost nightfall Wendell drove fast, reaching the rutted turnoff road not long after dark. Then down through the dense blackness of pine woods into the creek bottom, and left to where his headlights shone on the ruined hangar. There was no one, not yet. Late, a little late, he told himself, and standing beside his car listened into the dark.

Once he heard, breaking the soundless starless night, an owl somewhere, and later, just for an instant, a noise he took to be a motor approaching down the turnoff road. But this was thunder, the faintest grumble, from clouds where he afterwards saw throbs of lightning like bright blood in a vein. He thought he already knew they would not come.

Wendell did not know how long he stood there before this knowledge took the form of hair grown stiff at the back of his neck. Facing only the blind darkness he saw, all in a single crystalline flash, the black towering tree line spring to life. Then nothing, the dark—or nothing except in uncertain afterimage an impression of faces watching him from the woods. Finding the handle he quietly pulled the car door open. He drew a breath before he hit the starter.

Approaching the highway he slowed down for the first time and he actually stopped at the intersection. What held him back was the sudden question, Where? Not to his room. A glimpse of headlights made him stiffen. Well ahead of the lights he gunned the car onto the highway and driving fast kept on and on until he had a sense of familiar things sweeping past his windows. A house, a railroad crossing, a church with truncated steeple. Beyond these . . . ? Suddenly he knew where he would go.

The lights of the town and every light behind him, he passed the gate to Mr. Cartwright's farm. Beyond the orchard short of a little bridge twin tracks entered the highway. He followed them, ascending through plum thicket to where they turned and kept to the pasture fence. Without lights he could see, beyond a shadow gate, the dark place where the cabin stood. In fact the gate was not a gate but a plum bush screen between surviving posts. The cabin gone too, probably, a rotted rubble of boards and tin beneath the thicket. It did not matter. The car was shelter enough, a hiding place.

It did seem to matter. Wendell did not know exactly why but after a long time in which the impulse kept returning he got out of the car. A moment of lightning showed a sort of path. Two dozen steps, threading his way among the thorns, and he stood not far from a wall just paler than the night. Lightning came again, defining the darkness framed where a window had been. It was the empty window to his old room, close to his bed in the corner.

The bushes were not so thick in front and afforded glimpses of pasture and a distant light at Mr. Cartwright's house. But they grew where the porch had been, right up to the wall and the door that was not visible until he had picked his way past the thorny branches. One tall step up, higher than his hips. He stood on his old threshold staring at what his eyes could not see in the dark. Until lightning came. It flashed through gaps where wind had stripped whole sheets of tin from the roof. A rotted skeletal floor, a hole where the eating table used to stand. And litter of cans and old bird nests where floorboards were intact. He would sleep in the car.

This was his intention but the movement he made to follow it had a different issue. One slow step and then another, guided by lightning over the boards, took him as though away from the self he had left there on the threshold. To a doorway and on solider floor to the corner where rubble crunched under his feet. It was his place, his solace in the dark. A moment here and he would go back to himself.

But the moment continued and at a distance he drifted into the understanding that he was not on his feet anymore. Sitting propped in the corner, hugging warmth from his knees, he called on sleep in a kind of unuttered prayer.

Despite the cold, sleep did come. It was sleep as light as a veil, with whispering rain and hint of voices too remote to hear. He listened in his sleep, straining to catch the rumored sound of them. Finally—it seemed to be after the rain stopped—he was hearing them. He thought they were his brothers' voices, growing louder, growing so strident and painful in his head that he longed to stop his ears. Maybe he did: if so it was worse than useless. Not even human now the voices had a sound like fowl in anger, a demented scourging pitiless sound. When at last it waked him he found he was holding his head between his knees. There was somebody squatting on the floor nearby.

Knowing without seeing, Wendell did not lift his head. Water, measured drop by drop, fell on tin somewhere. On and on the drops were like minutes counting.

"You think to get off like this, boy?"

No answer came in Wendell's mind. The dropping minutes counted on. They might have been words spoken a long time ago.

"You been belonging to me all your life."

The voice receded in his mind and after a long succession of counting minutes Wendell believed he was alone again. But a shock followed this conclusion. The looming presence was visible to him by a single obscure detail. It was the mouth, with something peculiar about the way the lips had set themselves. He barely heard something, followed by a sensation on his cheek. In what he could never in later days

182

recall as merely a dream, the spittle hung there burning into his flesh.

The reasonable thing would have been to dismiss as dream or hallucination—another hallucination—his experience of that night in the cabin. And after he waked up to sunlight streaming through gaps in the roof and saw out in the pasture Mr. Cartwright's whiteface cows grazing, he found it easy enough to do this. The act of putting his fingers to his cheek seemed to accomplish the final purging of last night's illusion. In fact it inspired a feeling that for a little while afterwards resembled contentment.

But this was only a little while and what followed was a state of mind that at one intensity or another would continue to pursue him. Its essence was a kind of confusion like that when necessary light is unaccountably withdrawn. On his drive back to Turnbull he was more than once visited by a sense that familiar sights and memories both were merely distant, even if somehow disturbing, fictions.

Later that morning he talked with McCabe in one of the dim booths of a beer joint out on the Drayton road. At this second of their meetings, there was not yet any question of McCabe's confidence in Wendell. He simply looked like a man who, after an initial heat of excitement, had lost his prey. Following Wendell's slightly edited account he studied his cup of coffee for a while before he said anything else. Finally he said, "No show, then, huh? Spotted it some way. They got eyes where you wouldn't think. By now there won't even be any smoke left." Here he looked up at Wendell. "Unless you got something we can put our hands on."

Farrow, Wendell thought, his mind stopping on the vision of that face in moonlight. He saw how narrowly McCabe was watching him. McCabe said,

"You sure about Jason Farrow? What we need is some hard evidence. You got any of that?"

Wendell tried to think.

"He looks clean as a whistle. Unless you got something."
McCabe's eyes were obscurely netted with pink veins at the
corners.

Wendell had a thought. "There's the money he gave me.
A lot of it. I've got it hid."

McCabe considered a moment. "Okay." A little interest
had kindled in his eyes. "Could help. You get it for me.
Right away."

"The police," Wendell said. "In Turnbull. Doolin and the
other one, they work for him. He used them to set me up,
blackmail me." He thought of Doolin at his front door, the
knowing colluding face.

But McCabe was speaking. He wanted details, and Wendell, compelling his thoughts, set about answering the questions. Names, places, notions, all he could remember. It was
not very much. This, afterwards as he watched McCabe
close the notebook and slip it into his shirt pocket, was how
it struck Wendell now. At least what he had *said* was not
much. It was like a lie.

"Nothing else about Farrow, though, huh?"

Wendell tried, sifting among his thoughts. What remained
was once again Farrow's face in the moonlight. McCabe
waited, watching him narrowly. Wendell said, "You don't
know what he's like. He's . . . " Wendell stopped.

"Keep trying," McCabe said finally. "We got to have
something solid. Get that money. Meet me here at two
o'clock. Though it's not much use sneaking around anymore." McCabe paused. "I guess you'll be all right for now."
He got up out of the booth.

Wendell looked up at him but another thought interrupted. "What about the preacher?"

"We're checking. I'll let you know."

But then he did not turn away. Clearly the reason was
something in Wendell's face, and for an interval McCabe
waited. Then he was gone.

In fact it may have been close. As it seemed to Wendell
afterwards, the words already gathering in his throat had

been stopped only by McCabe's departure. His timely departure. For certainly McCabe was not the one. Turning this in his mind for a space Wendell arrived at a question that after still more thought produced no answer. Who, then, was the one? Trying to put it aside for now, he left and headed for Turnbull.

Half an hour later, in the stunning aftermath of what he had just discovered, McCabe's words came back to Wendell. "There won't even be any smoke left." Crouched inside the little door that opened under the house Wendell stared at the dark recess in the stone stanchion. He even put his hand in it again and found it, again, empty. No money, no box, nothing there at all. Smoke, he thought, becoming conscious finally of birdsongs and the muted grind of cicadas behind him in the noon sun. Nothing. His assurance about the hands—surely Cat Bird's black ones—that had preceded him here and left this recess empty was suddenly like a trick of imagination, a vision not to be credited. He passed some moments half-persuaded that he had dreamed that money.

By the time he approached and mounted the stoop to the kitchen door his clarity had returned. It did not stay. Seeing as he opened the screen door the identity of the person seated at the table was not a recognition so much as a magical event. It was as if the man had simply materialized there— Rathbone from his thicket of hair looking at Wendell across a table littered with pages of scrawl. This was Wendell's first impression, amended only seconds later by a quite different one. For what was strange in the daily fact of Rathbone seated here, gazing at Wendell, drawing breath to utter the thought flickering in his brain? This unimaginable summer, those nightmare things, had not really happened.

"You must see my notes, Wendell. It's all here, Blake revealed. I understand him now. My book will say it all." Rathbone's eyes, intensely bright, all but glared at Wendell. He was very high on something.

"The Bard, the Bard guided me, Wendell. I've got beyond the state of Generation. To Beulah at least, where re-

185

demption lives in imaginative vision. It's coming, I can feel it. I felt, in London . . . Ah London. I must go back to London, Wendell."

London. It was curious how the word came down in Wendell's mind, like a stab of daylight into a dream-filled room.

"They have . . . such things. Where can I get some good coke around here, Wendell?"

Wendell could only look back at him, noting how the bright eyes appeared sunken in Rathbone's head.

"Where is the car?"

But this, from the living-room door, was Alice speaking— a different Alice, he first thought, with hair cut short as if by pinking shears. No difference but the hair, though: the stunned look was the same old Alice. He gestured, murmuring, "Out there," and saw next the back of her head in silent stiff retreat through the living room. Then Rathbone's voice again.

"Poor Alice, no progress at all, a summer wasted. Condemned to Ulro, locked in static selfhood. Can you get me some coke?"

XX

It was Wendell's experience of the following days that ultimately gave him his best reasons for rejecting the explanations of common sense. These reasons, together with others from both his recent and his distant past, added up to a belief, practically a conviction, that he had been dealt with by forces of a superrational kind. Coincidences happened, all right. And a man's mind was capable of strange tricks and self-deceptions. But taking things all together he found it difficult not to believe that his soul had been the object of some discarnate form of manipulation.

A part of it was simply the way things happened to fall out, as in a pattern. Its center, in Wendell's conception, was another one of his face-to-face conversations with McCabe. Since their previous meeting two days had passed and Wendell had not got well seated across the table from him before he sensed a change. It was not something McCabe set out to reveal but after a little while the cause was clear enough. What he saw in McCabe's manner was doubt, and the object of the doubt was Wendell. The meeting was also one at which, in its later stages, he kept seeing himself as if through McCabe's eyes, defined by the image reflected there. These were moments of a kind already becoming familiar, when he seemed to get glimpses of a Wendell not easy to recognize.

Possibly McCabe's doubts had been awakened as early as the moment when Wendell reported the money stolen by Cat Bird. But it was the accumulation of things in their consistency that within a couple of days had all but demolished his faith in Wendell. The airstrip, both airstrips, that

Wendell had assumed would produce evidence enough revealed nothing substantial. One owner swore that the restoration out there was all news to him, and the other one that he, in the hope of selling the thing, had done the work himself. Both of them certainly bribed, McCabe had said, but the way he said it undercut his words. The fact that Wendell even knew about the airstrips clearly did not loom very large for McCabe. Because there was so much more that appeared to discredit Wendell's story.

Not one helpful fact came to light. McCabe, or McCabe and his colleagues, had checked on every detail, every name in Wendell's memory. Calvin Walls, ex-football player, existed, but without a blemish on his reputation. There was no trace of a Halloway, with his tiepin that said HOPE, or of anyone with the name of Evan McCauley. Cat Bird existed, all right, and Chief Doolin and Sheriff Grissom of Upjohn County. But what was there against them except for Wendell's claims? . . . And against Jason Farrow?

It was plain in McCabe's manner that here, the case of Farrow, was the point on which his confidence had seriously begun to fail. It was possible, of course: there had been such instances. But not *quite* such, Wendell gathered, in which not even a grain of suspicion attached to the man's good and respected name. Not yet, at least, McCabe told him, his doubt very clear in that moment. When he said this he surely was thinking of what he would soon spring on Wendell. It was an upcoming confrontation with the man himself.

Farrow had demanded it. The news about Wendell's charges had reached him, probably through Doolin, whom McCabe had thought it worth the venture to interrogate. In a question of his good name, Farrow publicly declared, he surely had the right to face his accuser. As if this was not enough, there was pressure also from McCabe. "There's a chance he might slip up. It's the only chance we got, you know." Wendell turned this in his mind. In the light of what he had seen by now, it amounted to a lie. Or half a lie at best. For it meant that McCabe would observe his performance with at least as much interest as Farrow's. What was Wendell to do? His thoughts of flight led straight into a darkness.

So, with McCabe at his side, he was there that morning in the little room that was Chief Doolin's office. What had he expected? Not, as his dreams had it, a toadlike figure squatted there or bulging eyes with cores of smoldering light. What he saw instead, with a muted shock of incredulity, was a heavy man in a business suit seated in a chair. No tinted glasses, nothing obscured the cool gray eyes that measured him. But still the fear was stuck in Wendell's throat, pinching the voice in which he had to answer.

With Doolin's desk and file cabinets against the wall behind it, one more person would have crowded the room. There was Doolin outspread on his swivel chair and Farrow erect on his own chair by the window. This was Farrow, in full daylight. In a business suit, blue seersucker, and wing-tipped shoes with a finish reflecting the sunlight. Even his voice, when he did speak, was a voice that Wendell could not recognize. But this was as true of his own voice, tight in his throat, failing him off and on, speaking things that seemed incredible. There were times when he barely stopped at the edge of the worst incredible things.

"Shit." This was Doolin. He had put his fat hands, loosely clenched, on the desk in front of him. "This here boy needs locking up on a funny farm. Don't you, boy?"

Just for a moment, hating him, Wendell looked back at the bright pig eyes. Again he was conscious of McCabe, relaxed in the chair next to his, observing him with that narrow disinterested gaze. Remotely now the sense of betrayal came back. But even if McCabe had believed him, what could he have said?

"Accusing a fine man like Mr. Farrow. Accusing ev'ybody. On *nothing*," Doolin said. "Me and Gummy talking about taking you to court, boy—trying to blacken our name." He looked at Farrow.

But Farrow was looking at Wendell, still looking, with

eyes that more than ever were a total stranger's eyes. Of the many such moments at their meeting that day, this was the one that Wendell's mind would always come back to. It was just as if an actual mist had fallen across the whole vista of his summer's memories.

Farrow's hands, drawing Wendell's gaze, adjusted the creases where the pants crossed his knees. Next he was standing up, looking not at Wendell but at McCabe, saying, "I'll just forget the whole thing. But I'd have this boy to a head doctor before I'd believe anything he says." Then he was gone.

In light of the notions that Wendell more and more came to hold about Farrow, he did not think that Farrow had asked for that meeting with the sole purpose of destroying his credibility in McCabe's eyes. Rather, he thought that it was Farrow's purpose also to deal with him, Wendell, personally. That up to a point Farrow accomplished both intentions was apparent afterwards, in the Grill, where Wendell sat with McCabe conversing between extended silences.

"Way too slick, that guy," McCabe said, his eyes on the coffee mug he kept tilting back and forth on the table. McCabe's little act, kept up without energy now, was all too obvious. More disconcerting and also curious to Wendell was a certain fitful consciousness that somehow he felt doubtful about his own story. Yet that man in the business suit, with the clear measuring gaze on Wendell, could only be the Jason Farrow of his memories and his dreams. Here again he was experiencing moments of a kind grown familiar, when the Wendell standing in his shoes seemed not to be fully himself. This particular experience of such moments eventually became the first cause of an opinion he continued to hold. It was that Farrow possessed a power to act on him this way.

In any case Farrow's twofold success that day seemed to be complete. Within hours the word about the meeting was out—put out certainly by Doolin. Disarmed as a threat and locked into the isolation that followed as expected, what was Wendell to do? There were times when he thought he knew what he should have done days ago, what he had repeatedly considered doing and could not do—not with the image of Joe's tortured face standing there in his mind. Impossible. Would even Joe believe him now? Not Joe, not anyone. So Wendell's dark secret would have to remain sealed up in his breast. This was Farrow's doing, his sorcery.

But this, the thought of sorcery—a thought that kept intruding on Wendell's mind—was in fact more than was needed here. To denote what could be explained as merely the subtler half of Farrow's design, he had only to consider a truth now made plain to him: that a festering guilt buried too long would end by consuming itself. Farrow understood this. In this knowledge he had contrived the means to draw an obdurate Wendell back into his power.

It might have happened: up to a point the design was working. That finally it did not work was because of an accident that Wendell believed was not an accident. He saw it as a mistake on Farrow's part. Just when it must have appeared to Farrow that nothing now could go awry, he went too far. Even the devil, Wendell thought, could grow impatient.

As he would see it, his progress back into Farrow's clutches had started within a day or two of that confrontation. It was nothing clearly perceptible, a drifting of the mind, a certain small abandonment of self that seemed a part of the change of weather. A succession of days carried the hint of fall, when the air in shady places and the shrill humming of dryflies in his head reminded him of distant things. On one such day he returned to a house not only cool at noon but softly resonant with a music he instantly recalled. Rathbone in a T-shirt lay sprawled on the sofa asleep, and Alice's scowl included him as they passed each other on the stairs. The car, something about the car. Waiting for him was a letter from the university, a reminder of classes to come and of empty student faces. His books. They were there on the shelves beside the chest of drawers. In addition he held fresh in his mind a comforting piece of news: that the preacher, though still absent, was unharmed. It seemed to Wendell that the light through the windows of his room entered from some changed angle of the sun.

There was a party that night, with faces he knew appearing early and late in the old random way, apparitions suddenly present and adrift in the mist of smoke. Old arguments resumed and fits of pointless laughter and music on the stereo that kept repeating itself. A woman named Donna wandered the house and returned and set out again, and Rathbone's voice in high discourse kept breaking clear of the others. "Ulro," Wendell heard. "Sterile negation." Until the time of stillness came. It was a room full of dreaming manikins, figures posed or maybe dropped on the floor and chairs and sofa. Upstairs at dawn the woman named Donna lay dead asleep in the hall.

This was how one day led to another and then another like it. Not that his mood could be described as one approaching tranquillity. But the sense of impending threat was almost gone and he kept experiencing that feeling of distance from himself. Sometimes it seemed that the procession of days through which he looked back on those events had begun already to diminish their stark shapes in his mind. For how could he do the only thing he was able to do about them? Recalling Joe at the kitchen table, he envisioned how it would be: the glazed, the devastated look of a man hit mortally hard. Though he would not, could not believe it now. Not Joe, not McCabe, not anyone at all . . . But here on more than one occasion Wendell's mind did pause. It was a thought about the preacher that left a sort of blank.

Even so, Wendell's conclusion was an honest one, however apt to mitigate remorse. For remorse was there, an undercurrent never entirely stilled. The worst of his moments were those when, arrested at his window, in the clutch of his own bound gaze he suffered the quietness of that house over there in the sun or the dark of night. Empty rooms, never a sound, not even a car in the drive. But what could he do? Always this question with its answer was there like a voice of rescue from his guilt. With relief as close to hand as this small question, it was easy to foresee the day when he would not need such relief.

But Farrow was impatient. This was what Wendell would come to believe, though nobody else had reason to think the appearance was not the truth itself. An accident, old wiring in an old and empty house. An accident, then, but all the same *Farrow's* accident. This once, however, his judgment of Wendell's response was seriously awry.

It happened in the middle of the night, flaring in Wendell's dreamless sleep like hell's own fire erupting. He opened his eyes on a room bleak and tremulous with light and for a moment lay there in bewilderment. He saw: it was Tricia's house. There was heat at his open window and out there beyond the hedge one great wallowing cone of flame thrumming and lashing its ultimate tip in the blackness of the sky. He thought there was something he should do, action he ought to take, and, snatching his clothes, plunged hands and feet into them. But what, what action? He stood in the heat watching, still watching when the siren approached and diminished and died away. Then only that sound like a ceaseless gale of hoarse and arid wind.

There were tall trees close to the fire. Stark limbs and trunks heaved in the glare, divesting themselves, casting flakes of burning leaves sucked up in the crest of flame. He thought, a thought that grew slowly in him, that those trees suffered pain, and he felt sorry for them.

It seemed to Wendell afterwards that this, his sorrow for the trees, was in the circumstances a trivial emotion. But he came to think that it was not, because its object was not really the trees and because it was not really, or only, pity. He could not define the emotion but he was able to recall what it was like. He would think of something inside him torn loose and painfully drawn from his body.

The house went up with astonishing speed. Two hours' time and it lay in flickering embers, in bursts and writhing tongues of flame, half-ringed by skeletal trees. Where the heat was tolerable idle firemen and a crowd by now thinned out stood talking or ambling past Wendell's spot beside the withered hedge. He was spoken to only once, by a voice he was slow to recognize. Yet it was Rathbone, standing close by in a robe of terrycloth that struck him above his bare knees.

"A new landscape to view," he said. One glance at the thicketed face and Wendell did not look again. "All purified. Sad, but it's not monuments we need. Just the earth, made new again." Wendell did not hear the rest of what he said and he did not even notice when Rathbone left him.

In time, except for two guardian firemen out in the front yard Wendell was alone. In time, though it did not seem like time. Above the lower trunks, limbs of the blackened trees extended themselves like pale trace-work in the shifting pall of smoke—all dead. Last life was in those sprouting and guttering tips of flame that bloomed sometimes and danced for a moment and died in the glowing rubble. Nearly gone. A night breeze came, roiling the smoke, and one dissolving plume there at the center bent and made a figure. Or so it was in Wendell's imagination. It was the shape of a staircase.

That was when it started, searing pain, like a wound spread open by degrees in some vague part of his body. In pain like a flare he saw Tricia's face, death-white, with white lips speaking and making no sound, flee past him down the stairs. That face in the kitchen, waiting, a time full of a mockingbird's song as raucous as a jay's. Then the sound from above, the thump. "I think she fell," Tricia said.

XXI

Wendell never did believe that he had merely imagined those words spoken in Tricia's voice. They were starkly clear in his memory, all right, but this was not memory speaking. He not only started, he wheeled half around to face the hedge and the shrubbery humped in the gloam. Surely that was her voice. It was more likely that what he afterwards saw, however lasting the impression, was in fact imagined. In the low shifting pall of smoke, illumined and dark by turns, the tremulous figures of both those women kept appearing, sometimes looking at him and sometimes not. He did know that whenever he thought they were looking at him he lowered his eyes or turned his face away.

It must have been about an hour before dawn when Wendell pushed his way back through the hedge into Rathbone's yard. Then he was in the kitchen, seated at the table under the burning bulb. A question kept getting lost in his mind. It had to do with an action, something evasive that kept approaching but would not reveal itself. When it came to him it seemed to be in consequence of the movement that brought him to his feet. Evidently his taking matches from the box on top of the stove was part of his intention.

It was still not clear when he emerged from the thicket of shrubbery into Farrow's yard and approached the dark back porch. He saw no light in the high window, only the cupola defined against the failing stars. Then came the chill he had known before, like wind through hackles grown stiff on the back of his neck. This stopped him. If his intention was to set this place on fire, it was not enough. One deep breath and he put his foot on the steps.

There was a moment of illusion when Wendell saw him in his chair. Approaching the door he lifted his hand to knock, and let it fall. He reached and touched the knob and, closing his fingers, turned it, in vain. What he did next, suddenly with a violent thrust of his foot, left him standing there in a chaos of echoes and shattered glass falling around him. In the following seconds he seemed to be deaf and fancied that the cause of it was a gunshot from within. The silence persisted. After a time the blood leaped back to his heart.

Wendell never thought that what he did on impulse was any part of the intention with which he had set out. It had simply come upon him that only an act of naked and irrevocable defiance could ever be enough. In fact, as he would later think, the mere interval of a day in which to gain distance on this night's event would likely have set him again on his former course. Even as he stood facing the door his foot had shattered, it seemed that already his courage was wavering. Until the silence persuaded him that Farrow was not in the house. Then he entered.

In the dark kitchen, where he stopped, his assurance began to fail. The silence confirmed neither one thing nor the other and his decision at last to move on was like a step into nothing. A few such steps and he faced the open door to the little parlor where he had sat with Farrow. The bulk of the desk seemed to be visible. So for just the space of a breath did the man himself seated in a chair.

In the empty living room first dawn blued the windowpanes. At last through an arched doorway the single bottom step of an invisible staircase came abruptly into view. He barely paused this time. Approaching he put a foot on the step and slowly began to climb.

On the dark landing he faced a door barely defined in the wall. This was when he began to smell something, a foul sweat-stink touched with smoke that must have come from his own body. But the door: a hesitant push, then a decisive one and there in a twilight tinctured with red an empty room appeared. Not this, some other room? Yet there directly opposite him was the high window where he was accustomed to see the nightlight. Not quite an empty room. Two guarded steps across the threshold made just visible the small table with a lamp by the window and in a far corner what looked to be a cot. Nothing more, nothing at all in the room. Except this tinctured dusk.

Or was he wrong? He thought it was the smell, the stink of himself, that brought the question into his mind. Because he had somehow stopped being sure that it came from his own body. This was a thought that invaded him like a chill, freezing him where he stood, producing finally a single definite impression in his head. Or, rather, *on* his head, the right side, because it was on that side that he felt a presence. The impression was so strong that he could not look—not yet, not for a long time. It was only after the light increased in the room that he was able to turn his eyes and look toward the wall where there was not anything to see.

The light had reddened almost into day. It entered through a trapdoor in the ceiling, from above in the cupola where tinted panes filtered the growing dawn. Full day coming on. He turned toward the door, and stopped. There were matches in his pocket. On the cot were bedclothes. Better still, on the walls, peeling sheets and tags of dried-out paper. He stepped to the wall. He struck a match.

Wendell never knew with any clarity what happened. He remembered striking that match and lifting the flame to one of those tags of peeling wallpaper. He thought he had heard a sound close by but it was almost as one thing with what issued from it. If this was a blow to his head, as was literally probable, it did not leave his memory with any recollection of the impact. Instead it seemed that the matchflame simply erupted and burst in his face with a violence that set him backwards off his feet. From the blurred aftermath he retained a sense of his body cruelly handled, shaken as if in the grip of jaws, and hurled. There was one final disembodied moment. That was the tiny interval of his fall from that high window to the ground.

It was more than a day later when Wendell, in a hospital bed, regained consciousness. Or full consciousness, rather, for there had been interludes when he hovered just at the surface long enough to take in certain things. Never much and hardly ever clearly—voices, a few words, people like shadows standing over him. One such interlude kept returning and after the known or apparent facts in his case were reported to him he got it sorted out.

It was in Farrow's yard when he lay on the ground under that window. His memory could not produce even shadow figures standing over him or any distinct words. But there were voices, very low, two of them. He knew from the first that one was Farrow's and he soon recognized that the other belonged to Cat Bird. It was not hard to tell that they were in a discussion. Much harder to tell was how Wendell knew with such perfect certainty the import of the discussion. But he knew, even then with a chill around his heart, that it was a question of his fate. How it was answered he would not have known except that he was here in the hospital and that he had criminal charges against him.

There was a cast on his right arm and a sheath around his hips because one was broken and bandage over part of his face. But the worst of it was his eyes: something behind his eyes was damaged. Not only was his vision impaired, there were times when he could barely see at all. It might heal itself, the doctor told him. There was nothing to do but wait. So this was what Wendell set himself to do. There was not anything else, not that he could think of without remorse or a never quite stilled anxiety. A prisoner on a bed in this white room, he waited for those intervals when he could see with decent clarity the yellowing leaves of a sweetgum tree outside his window.

Only a few days had passed when Wendell received a

piece of news expected to be heartening to him. The neat buxom nurse brought it in with a smile that was not returned. Farrow had dropped the charges against him. The question Why, with the old dark anxiety in its wake, came instantly to mind. He studied the matter for a while and thought he had found the answer. His answer was confirmed on the following day when he had a visitor.

The man was a shrink. He did not announce it, he merely said that he was a doctor, Dr. Jarman, and cheerfully invited himself to sit down in a chair by Wendell's bed. Just for a little talk, which he steered with a deftness that did not for long disguise his purpose. It came down to the question of Wendell's motive, about which the doctor pretended to be no more than idly curious. The youthful face, with frank blue eyes, had a pleasant expression. There was a sort of hiatus when all of it, the whole incredible sequence of his deeds, came to order in Wendell's mind. With eyes still fairly clear for now, he considered the pleasant face observing him. It was not a face to permit so much as a hint at disbelief. Wendell looked through the window at the tree out there and said, "I'm not crazy." He said it almost distantly, knowing his words would have no weight in the judgment he foresaw.

A term of confinement, maybe, for observation? Just as when he had considered prison a certainty for him, he viewed the possible outcome here entirely without distress. At least this would be something in his future. There was a strange irony in the thought that followed this one. It was that Farrow by casting him out had emptied his life of the only meaning it had.

He had trouble sleeping and he spent much of his time waiting for the tree outside his window to become clearly visible again. The rest of the time he spent dodging thoughts that as often as not were too quick for him. One day when his eyes were at their dimmest he heard a familiar voice speak to him. He turned his head and saw a shadow, Rathbone's shadow. An unlikely presence. It was vaguely astonishing that Rathbone with his Blake-besotted brain should have heard the news at all, much less thought to act upon it.

"A little bad luck, eh Wendell?"

He must have expected some details, because he stood in silence for an uncharacteristically long time. It struck Wendell that in all his abortive thoughts about confessing, never once had Rathbone crossed his mind.

"A little," Wendell finally, faintly said.

A moment more and Rathbone gave it up. "You know me, Wendell, I never pry. And I never listen to Rumor's voice. I know you and that's all I need to know. To see *through*, not *with* the eye. You remember that bit of Blake, don't you, Wendell?"

Wendell just gazed at what he could see of Rathbone.

"That's the *poet's* vision. They thought Blake was mad too. But I know your spirit, Wendell. You soar on your own wings. The fool's reproach is a kingly title."

Wendell had not planned to say it and after he did he lay there as if something he had dropped would explode when it struck. He said, "I killed the old lady . . . me and Tricia."

The shape of Rathbone was merely still: his face was solid shadow. But after a space his head moved. "Yes," he said and, later, his voice a little muted, "but I was wondering about that Farrow person. Do you think he really is a dealer?"

It took Wendell a long moment to understand.

"Do you think if I got in touch with him secretly . . . ?" He paused. "It's mostly for Alice. She's practically an addict now, you know."

Wendell turned his face away and listened while Rathbone sputtered down at last to a conclusion. Not quite a conclusion. From the door, barely pausing, he said, "Expect poison from still water, Wendell."

On the day when a quite different kind of visitor appeared Wendell was asleep. It was a light sleep and he had consciousness of the presence before he could get his eyes open. What made him violently start was not the obscurity of the figure, a condition he was accustomed to, but that there was so much of it: in his first perception it might have been standing with its head against the ceiling. Even after the skip in time when he knew who the figure was, the pace of his blood did not appreciably slow down.

"How you feeling?"

Wendell tried for a reply but he did not make any sound. His vision was good enough, or had become so, that he could discern the movement of lips when the man spoke again.

"Name's Sears. I met you at Mrs. Harker's funeral." When he got no response he said, "I seen you around before, sometimes, too. You're one of Hap Corbin's boys, ain't you?"

He thought, Yes, as if it was an uncertain fact. Then he said it audibly. "Yes." Details of the man's figure began to be visible.

Sears moved. Bending he placed the chair and sat down a step away from Wendell's bed. He appeared to be scrutinizing Wendell. He said, "Nurse told me about your eyes. They getting any better?"

"Not much," Wendell murmured. His heart was quieter now.

"Pray it'll happen. I'll do the same." He was silent for a time. Then, "That fellow McCabe told me about it. Said you come to warn me and all. He told me a lot of things." Sears waited a moment. "He said you mostly made them things up in your head."

Wendell turned his face away. Was it vision returned or old nightmares that had pictured the gaze trained on him?

"Was they just lies?"

"No. They were true. All of them."

"That about Jason Farrow?"

"Yes. All of it."

"Look at me and say that."

Wendell was slow but he turned his head. Yes, he could see, and what he could see were eyes intent without menace. Meeting them he said, "It's true about Farrow. All of it's true."

The eyes blinked and just for a second wandered. They

were large eyes and yellow-flecked but not as his memory had it. Their intentness came back. "They say it's all in your head, you know."

"I know. That's what he wants. Farrow. He made it look like that."

Sears's gaze wandered again and came back. "There ain't no proof of that."

"It's true, though. Nobody knows what he is. But me." Then because it stood up in his mind he said, "You never were in my house, were you? A week or so after the funeral? I just dreamed you were. That you knew what I did." He stopped. Just why he knew he had made a mistake was not quite plain to him yet.

"Mrs. Harker's funeral, you mean?" Sears paused. "Naw. I don't even know where your house is." The mistake was reflected in his expression. "You had to of dreamed that one."

Wendell turned his head and looked out the window at the tree. The turning leaves, all its features, were very clear in his eyes.

As from a distance he heard Sears say, "You want to tell me what you dreamed?"

"It was because of what I did," Wendell murmured. "It's no use telling you, though."

"I'm willing to listen," Sears said.

Wendell drew a breath. He gazed at the tree and let the words come out.

Given the work he did, neither his limp nor the fact that he was still partly blind was too much of a handicap. He could help to load a truck and raise a tent; and to distribute hand-bills on a street corner or to pass a collection plate at a meeting did not require much in the way of vision. Sears would have done the driving in any case, and where reading was necessary Sears could do it well enough. Wendell wished for the day, and that it would come soon, when he could read again. But he could wait. Somehow he had become satisfied to wait. There was nothing wrong with his hearing and he discovered that there were a great many sounds in the world to which he had never paid much attention.

For the weeks following his decision Wendell had thought that such a life was not to be borne. Days at the trailer alone or in Sears's company were days passed mainly in silence, with birdsongs and the passing of a car once in a while and water running in the creek. There was little talk between them: necessary words and sometimes Sears's voice reading aloud from the Bible for Wendell's benefit. And there were the trips, the meetings, between which their days at the trailer were merely breathing spaces.

But the meetings themselves were the events that threatened his resolution. Seated on his chair at the back of the tent, assistant to the Sower, he was almost grateful for the hours when his vision made shadows of all those spent innocent faces harkening to the Word. There were times when the Word, the impassioned words that spread the Word, made him think that he wished his hearing was at least as dim as his sight. More than once, noticing a figure indistinct in the light outside the tent, his old rage came back. That was himself out there, his early self beginning to quake in the terror of hellfire. This ogre holding his Bible on high was a fraud, a skinner of sheep.

Wendell was wrong, as ought to have been clear to him from the start. He would not forget those particular minutes that day in the hospital, the grave eyes reading his face, in turn appalled and not appalled. Sears could believe it because he had believed harder things and because evil was the first of the stories in his book. But he also believed the rest of it and, seeing how things stood with Wendell, undertook to save another soul.

But this, like his final acceptance of Wendell's story, was not the decision of a single hour. He had his uncertainties for a while and other questions for Wendell on other visits. Even for Sears one thing was very hard. Looking into Wendell's face, "I keep thinking about Miss Tricia," he said. "But if she done that, to her own self . . ."

His pause became a silence that was more than a silence for Wendell. If there was any moment when his story appeared in a suddenly different light, it was here—as if this light had passed to him from the eyes that were fastened on him. This was what he imagined, turning his face aside. In any case it was in that one flash of experience that the word *appalling* received its final definition for Wendell. As though the gaze turned on him was his own, he saw himself but not, somehow, himself—a self too small in stature, shrunken and burnt-dry-looking and pitiless in the face, that was and was not him. The image afterwards kept no precisely fixed character in his mind. What remained entirely fixed was the feeling with which he had received it. *Hate* would have to serve to designate the feeling, though he never had felt hate like that toward any person or thing.

Wendell often wondered if in some impossible way Sears had indeed shared in that devastating flash of vision. There must have been times when, remembering the old lady, his benefactor, he looked at Wendell in some such light as that. If so, it never showed. There was never even the kind of harassment about Jesus that Wendell at first had kept expecting. A few words, or hints discreetly uttered. The extent of it was his saying to Wendell on two or three occasions, "Just get your heart right. He don't never fail."

Wendell thought about this and was doubtful. He felt this way especially at times when he went into Turnbull or passed through with Sears in the truck. Sometimes in passing he was able to see the space with standing chimneys that framed his memory of Tricia's house. And once at the intersection he stopped for a long look up Rudd Street to where it abutted on Farrow's high hedge. The house appeared unchanged, rising from its banks of green, its white cupola as tall as the treetops. It was the same and *he* was the same, with his prospering car lot and the town's respect and his cold vigils on that back porch in the glaze of moon or starlight—lethal in his stillness. It may have been that this was the main source of Wendell's doubtfulness.

Sometimes, and more and more often, he would hear reports that brought Farrow with a sort of violence into his mind. It made no difference that often these were reports of events far removed from Turnbull and Bliss County. He would think of Cat Bird, whom he had once or twice glimpsed in the car lot polishing cars, and of that time years ago when he had asked Cat straight out who the Big Man was. He could still see Cat's face uplifted in mock rhapsody to the sky and hear his words about the stars and the lightning falling. The memory was the very image of an anxiety that visited Wendell all too often.

One day in the humming crystal stillness of late November he borrowed Sears's old car and in spite of his vision drove to the state Home For The Infirm. The news at the desk was what he had hoped for. Carefully winding his way along the hall among the desiccated figures in wheelchairs who seemed to watch him without eyes or gestured urgently, he discovered his father in the doorway to his room, his chair positioned exactly across the threshold. The old man looked up at him noncommittally when Wendell bent to push him back inside and continued to watch him when Wendell sat down on the bed in the sterile room.

As often in the past, there did not appear to be anybody at all at home. Here in sunlight from the window Wendell could see him well enough. The old man's pale eyes appeared to be without much life but this had been true always. His hands, though tender-looking, were hands that Wendell would have recognized among thousands, with loose bony fingers lying on his knees. That his mouth hung open was nothing new, and neither was the unwholesome pink replacing the old burnt-red of his face and neck. Wendell finally said, "Hi, Pa," but his father just looked at him.

Words of some kind seemed necessary and Wendell started to talk. It did not matter what. "The hay's all in the barn," he said and talked a little about how heavy the bales were and about the cows getting hungry and about the winter pasture. And all the time the old man's washed-out eyes were looking into Wendell's face.

There was a sudden difference. Like the very definition of whatever it was that Wendell had been waiting for, it happened. His father lifted his right hand. With index and second finger held uncertainly apart, he put the hand to his mouth as though he held a reefer in it. For a while after that, because of the gratitude welling up in him, Wendell could not see at all.